BAIT
& SWITCH

Mayfield Mystery #1

D1557489

Jerusha Jones

CHAPTER 1

His giant blue-gray eye bulged in the peephole, the red squiggly veins in his sclera pulsing. I held my breath, then nearly jumped out of my skin as the door beneath my fingertips thumped with another volley of determined knocking.

"Mrs. Sheldon. We know you're in there." He spoke in a low voice, as though his mouth was pressed against the crack between the door and the frame.

I squinted through the peephole again, this time to see a badge—an ID card?—waved across the distorted scope of my view.

"FBI. If you don't open up soon, we're going to collect a bunch of spectators out here on the lawn. Not something you want, I'm thinking."

I didn't care what he thought I wanted. I exhaled and spun so my back pressed against the door. What I really wanted was my husband of fourteen hours to return.

Skip had promised, "I won't be long, honey." He'd kissed me on the forehead while sliding his arms back into his linen suit jacket sleeves. Then he'd gone out, and I'd been left standing in the middle of one of El Escondite's luxury bungalows surrounded by our luggage and staring at a closed door.

The same door rattled again, and I leaped away from it. "One minute—a few minutes. Please?" My voice shook, and I tried again, louder. "It's late. I need to dress. Five minutes?"

"Five minutes," Mr. Badge echoed into the crack. "Hurry up."

I fled for the bedroom and the piles of clothing I'd just started unpacking. I'd figured the silky negligee and skimpy robe I had on were all I was going to need tonight. I dug through my suitcase and found a pair of jeans, a T-shirt, the appropriate underwear.

My hands shook as my mind raced through scenarios. Skip had been injured—fallen off an embankment into the sea, hit by a car in a crosswalk, held at gunpoint—that one made my heart stop. Skip had the net worth to make kidnapping appealing. But he was strong—he wouldn't go without a fight. A knife fight with banditos? What else could it be?

But why was the FBI at my door? They didn't follow ambulances around, informing the family, especially not in Cozumel, Mexico.

I hopped on one foot, trying to pull a sling-back espadrille onto the other. I'd bought these shoes for our honeymoon, thinking they'd be good for long walks through El Mercado and the side-street shops while holding hands with Skip. I closed my eyes and gulped a deep breath. Maybe the nice man outside would explain everything—a simple misunderstanding, a knock on the wrong door in the wee hours of the morning.

But he knew my name—my new name.

A quick check through the peephole showed two cheap suits standing under the bright porch light, poking their phone screens. Just like the television shows—the FBI always comes in pairs. I squared my shoulders and opened the door.

The lead guy's head popped up. He wrapped a warm hand around my elbow. "The car's at the curb."

"Who are you?"

"Special Agent Mick Jordan. And Patrick Moreno, my partner." He gestured toward the man who took up position on my other side.

"Are you here about Skip? Is he okay? You'd at least tell me that, wouldn't you?" At the hard look on both men's faces, I bit my lip and whispered, "Please?"

"It's best if we save the questions for when we get to the office," Agent Jordan said.

They propelled me through the sticky night, cutting across the curves of the resort's meandering lighted path to an idling dark sedan. Agent Jordan followed me into the backseat while Agent Moreno folded his bulky body into the front passenger seat.

The unintroduced driver gunned the car into the sparse traffic. He had a pale strip of skin between his haircut and shirt collar. Yet another non-local.

I twisted my purse strap between my fingers, rubbing it hard the way my housecleaner, Rosemary, parses her rosary beads. I'm not Catholic, but having something to hold onto right now seemed an absolute necessity.

Five minutes later we pulled up in front of a bougainvillea-covered wall in what was clearly a residential neighborhood.

"Office?" My voice quivered.

"For now." Agent Jordan let me exit the car unassisted then pushed open the silent wrought iron gate.

The house was typical—whitewashed adobe walls and barred windows with a heavy wood door. We stepped into a tiled foyer and around the corner into a sparsely furnished sitting room. And by sparsely, I mean a few metal folding chairs and a card table crammed with electronic equipment and laptops. A couple empty duffel bags lay crumpled in a corner. Not exactly hospitable, and certainly not the usual government agency office.

A very large, very white, barefoot man wearing a Madras plaid shirt that stretched taut across his beer belly and khaki cargo shorts slouched in one of the chairs—the only one of the four men who even came close to fitting in with the local tourist population. He glanced up for a fraction of a second, one bushy gray eyebrow raised. "Still got nothin'," he grunted. His right hand flicked a computer mouse, and his eyes returned to scanning the screens.

"In here, Mrs. Sheldon." Agent Jordan led me through a galley kitchen that looked and smelled the way I imagine a frat house would—partially empty take-out cartons, tipped soda cans, scrunched plastic bags, even a bunch of brown-spotted bananas swarming with fruit flies. I never got near those places in college for precisely this reason. I pressed a hand to my nose and almost tripped on the back of Agent Jordan's heels in my haste.

The dining room looked more normal, and unused, with heavy, carved wood chairs lined up around a refectory-style table. Agent Jordan pulled out a chair and pointed me into it.

He peeled off his suit jacket and slung it over the back of another chair. "Something to drink?"

I shook my head. I pressed my knees together and clenched my purse on my lap, trying to suppress my trembling. I had a horrible, irrational thought that the less DNA I deposited, the better. I didn't know the first thing about how FBI agents work, but this crew seemed shady and poised to clear out in a hurry.

Agent Jordan returned with a steaming Styrofoam cup and dropped into his chair with a heavy sigh. "Your husband's gone."

I scowled. He had to drag me out of my comfortable bungalow to tell me something we both already knew?

"You wanna tell me where?" He loosened his tie and ran a hand through his stiff hair.

"What do you mean? Is he hurt? Have you checked the hospitals?" I pitched forward on the edge of my chair. "Why are you interested in my husband's health?"

"Believe me, lady, I'm not. He's in a high-risk occupation. It'd just be nice to have a body as proof—that's all."

CHAPTER 2

"Body?" I spluttered. "He's a businessman. Car wash franchising. If that's dangerous, well then—this is ridiculous." I sprang out of my chair. "I'll check the hospitals myself."

"Sit down, Mrs. Sheldon." Agent Jordan half rose and pointed at my empty chair. "Sit. Why don't you just call him?"

"I can't." The past few hours at the bungalow, I'd been trying to make myself useful, and that included finding Skip's phone between sections of the previous day's *Wall Street Journal* in his soft-sided carry-on briefcase. He must have dropped it in there when we'd boarded the charter jet. He's notorious for losing small but important items like his car keys and inhaler.

"He didn't take his phone with him, did he?"

I shook my head and sank back onto the chair. "How do you know?"

"GPS. We've been tracking him for a while."

"Why?"

Agent Jordan squinted at me. "I think the question is how much do you know?"

"Is this about the Indonesian orphanage fund that turned out to be a cover for the Jemaah Islamiyah terrorist group?"

Agent Jordan choked on a sip of coffee.

"We figured it out in time and halted the transfer," I blurted. "So technically we didn't do anything illegal."

Agent Jordan rubbed at the brown spray pattern on the front of his white shirt. His fingers were thick and stubby. One nail had a black spot from a run-in with a hammer or other similar injury.

I clamped my jaw closed. I might have just said too much.

Agent Jordan fished in the pocket of his suit jacket, came up with a small leather-bound notebook and a pen. He made a show of clicking the pen and writing a few lines. "Anything else you want to tell me?"

"No." I spun my wedding ring on my finger. It was too heavy and too big. Skip had promised to get it resized when we returned home. I'd told myself I would become accustomed to the huge emerald bauble surrounded by diamonds. I glanced up at Agent Jordan. "This is my husband we're talking about. What danger is he in? Why did you say 'body'?"

Agent Jordan puffed out a long breath and propped his elbows on the table. He had dark pouches under his eyes. "You know you married the biggest money launderer west of the Mississippi, right?"

I snorted. Then I got the giggles. It was just so absurd. "Skip can't balance his own checkbook. He's full of good intentions, but that doesn't translate to spreadsheets—which is how we met in the first place."

Agent Jordan pinched the bridge of his nose and spoke from behind his hand. "I might be inclined to believe that *you* believe what you just said. But if you knew your husband better, you wouldn't find this so funny."

"He hired me to oversee his portfolio of non-profits. I'm the one who makes sure his foundation isn't taken advantage of—that our grants go to well-managed organizations with stellar track records. We check." I thumped my purse on the table. "My team and I make surprise visits. We audit their books. We interview the people who benefit from their services. I personally sign off on every approved request." Sweat trickled between my shoulder blades, and my temples were pounding. "I don't think you'll find a better-run philanthropic organization— even west of the Mississippi."

My sarcasm was wasted on Agent Jordan. His face remained as impassive as a bowl of congealed oatmeal. "I'm talking about his for-profit enterprises."

"I'm sure Robbie—Robert Van Buren, the company's controller—can set things straight, if you'll just talk to him. You're evading the issue. Where is my husband?" My voice pitched up an octave.

"I don't know. I told you that."

"Did he vanish before your very eyes or what?" I shouted. So much for my veneer of civility. My mother would be appalled. Yelling at a government employee is not proper form.

"Pretty much." His voice was so quiet, I wasn't sure I'd heard him correctly.

I swallowed and started blinking fast.

Agent Jordan rose and plodded from the room. He returned with a roll of toilet paper. "Sorry. I realize this is your wedding night, and it's not turning out the way you expected."

I blew my nose. "Please tell me what you do know."

"He exited the bungalow at 8:23 p.m. He borrowed one of the resort's golf carts, drove down the walkway to the beach entertainment area—" Agent Jordan glanced up from his notes.

I nodded. He meant the string of grass huts that festively shroud open bars where the resort's guests can obtain all manner of mind-numbing beverages and spend the day and well into the night telling themselves they are having a fabulous time when in fact they are smashed-into-a-lounge-chair-face-first drunk.

"He parked, walked straight to the first hut—the Pineapple Express—and ordered a whiskey. When his drink arrived, so did four other men. We know who three of them are. They stepped away from the hut, had a short conversation, then a scuffle. One man was kidney-punched hard enough to drop to his knees."

I gasped. "He *is* hurt. Why didn't you do something?"

Agent Jordan held up a finger. "That's when the agents watching moved in. Tiki torches don't provide the best illumination. Like you, they thought it was your husband getting roughed up. It wasn't."

I scowled and opened my mouth. At Agent Jordan's warning look, I snapped it shut.

"The men scattered, leaving behind their injured companion—the one we don't have an ID for, and he's not talking. Your husband fled with the others. Given who they are and the kind of working relationship they have, we're not convinced he went willingly. We're not sure they have enough reasons to keep him alive."

"But you know where he is and who's holding him." I balanced precariously on the edge of my seat. "You can go after them."

"It's not that easy. We know the who, but not the where. And these three men—they work for completely different criminal organizations. If they were coordinating tonight, it would be an unprecedented political move in the underworld. Either they've turned renegade and formed a new coalition or your husband royally screwed over the groups they represent and they've united for revenge."

I forgot how to breathe. I wanted to scream, to pound on the table and bellow that this is not the man I married, that there must be some terrible mistake, that Skip is kind and generous and gentle and nearsighted and asthmatic, for goodness' sake. Not the sort of man who keeps company with criminals, let alone steals their money.

As though he could read my mind, Agent Jordan said, "These guys are picky about their money. Billions."

"You think my husband was using our honeymoon as cover for illegal activity?" I croaked.

"I know he was." Agent Jordan sighed heavily. "Your continued presence in Cozumel would not be helpful. You need to call the charter company and tell them you're going home early. The honeymoon's over."

~oOo~

I spent the next few hours repacking, pacing, pressing against the sliding glass doors to the patio and ocean beyond hoping that my husband would walk up the path, apologetic and worried because he'd been detained by some fluke accident. And then he'd tell me that the FBI was delusional or I'd had a really bad dream.

My hands ached from clenching into fists, half-moons from my fingernails permanently imprinted in my palms. I didn't dare say anything out loud. I couldn't talk to myself as I normally would. Every dark spot in the wallpaper and shadow in the exposed-beam rafters turned into a tiny camera lens or microphone in my imagination.

If the FBI was tracking Skip's phone—which was still on the kitchen counter next to his briefcase—then what else were they doing? Skip had made the reservation for this particular bungalow a month ago. They'd have had plenty of time to bug it.

The call to the jet charter service was torture. The agent tried to sound comforting and understanding, but I could tell she was biting her tongue not to ask why we were returning from our honeymoon so soon. Then I had to tell her there'd be only one passenger. Talk about a pregnant silence. She repeated that the bar on the plane would be fully stocked—anything I wanted—and, another pause, was I okay?

I whimpered a *yes* because I've been trained to maintain socially acceptable behavior at all times, and this includes bald-faced lies. I come from a world where people are admired for their ability to pretend even when everyone around them knows that's exactly what they're doing. I hung up.

I debated leaving Skip's luggage in storage with the concierge, but that would involve explanations and dragging the suitcases past the FBI agent installed in a rattan rocking chair on the front stoop.

Agent Jordan had insisted on having the black suit and sunglasses-clad young man watch over me and openly escort me to the airport, just so the bad guys would know that the FBI knew—what, I wasn't sure. Not a bodyguard. Just sending a message in case anyone was watching.

Which really meant that Agent Jordan in particular and maybe the rest of the FBI didn't trust me. They were watching *me* to see what I would do. The terrible thing was I had absolutely no idea what to do, except cry. And I wouldn't give them the satisfaction.

~oOo~

One of the great things about chartered flights is the opportunity to miss the mess—the long lines through customs and security, witnessing tourists behaving badly, being crammed together with sweaty, overweight people whose ideas of personal space and hygiene are considerably different from my own.

A be-tasseled customs official banged his stamp on my passport and handed it back with a brilliant smile.

An air steward in a set of dress whites that would make the preppy tennis set proud wrangled my luggage onto a cart, leaving me free to climb the rolling stairs into the gleaming Learjet. I felt no need to wave goodbye to the FBI agent in his broad stance on the far side of the chain-link fence. A stiff ocean breeze called his bluff, whipping his pant legs against his skinny calves.

I sank into a smooth leather recliner and closed my eyes. I'd have a few hours of anonymous oblivion in this quiet, cool cabin. And I needed a plan before the wheels touched down again.

CHAPTER 3

Actually, I needed two plans. One based on the FBI being right and another based on my being right—right about Skip.

The only thing I agreed with Agent Jordan about is that my presence in Cozumel would be counterproductive. If anyone can find a missing man, it's the FBI. I, as a distraught, half-crazy, brand-new wife wouldn't be able to do much except weep in the visitor's chairs in the offices of various local law enforcement officials and make impassioned pleas on television.

I had neither the money nor clout to prod anyone into faster action regarding Skip's disappearance. Agent Jordan had hinted that I should make myself available for receiving a ransom request.

If Skip was alive, he could direct his kidnappers where to find me. But I wasn't keen to be in the public eye. And I figured we both needed his business to go on as usual which meant not blathering our problems all over the place.

The first issue to tackle was the legitimacy of the FBI's claims—money laundering. As soon as we were at cruising elevation, I grabbed a bottle of water from the mini-fridge and dialed Robbie.

Voice mail. I left a cryptic message about the company's financial records, and that Skip was unavailable so Robbie had better talk to me or else.

Then I called Skip's number two, the vice president and operations manager of Turbo-Tidy Clean, LLC. It was Sunday. Leroy would have to find Robbie and enforce his presence in the office until I got there. I wanted a look at the accounts before the FBI confiscated them.

"What?" Leroy yelled. "You talked to the FBI?"

"Isn't that what law-abiding citizens usually do? My husband's missing," I shouted back.

"I thought you had more sense, Nora."

My stomach tightened into a hard knot. "Skip's been kidnapped—or killed. Did you miss that part?"

"You need to clam up and lay low. As the spouse, they can't make you testify. I'll call you back." Leroy clicked off.

I pulled my knees up and wrapped my arms around them, burying my face between the knobby joints. No, no, no, no.

I'd expected blustering disbelief from Leroy, adamant assertions of Skip's innocence and despair about his possible condition. This could not be happening.

All the aspects of Skip's philanthropic efforts under my control were clean—no question—and the foundation kept a separate office. Maybe there was still some hope. I called the personal number of Clarice, my executive assistant, who just might be at the office on a Sunday, given her workaholic habits.

"Girl, it's your honeymoon. I'm going to beat you over the head with a two-by-four if you don't hang up this second. We aren't on fire or dying." Clarice's scratchy, ex-smoker's voice crackled in my phone. She now has a permanent Juicy Fruit aura to replace the nicotine.

I almost dissolved, then the words came in a deluge. I told her everything.

When I finished, she was quiet too long.

An air steward poked his head around the partition from the galley. "Sandwich?" he mouthed.

I shook my head and waited until he disappeared again. "Talk to me," I whispered into the phone. "What are you thinking?"

"I'm making a to-do list," Clarice growled. "Take the battery out of Skip's cell phone."

I fumbled in my tote bag. "Done."

"But hang onto the phone. It'll be interesting later to see who's been trying to contact him."

"Do you think he's guilty?"

"I'm as shocked as you are—stupefied—but I think we'd better act on that supposition. I'll call you back in a little bit. Hold tight." Clarice hung up.

Was I an idiot? The evidence was pointing to my complete inability to judge a man's character.

But Skip and I had been so well suited. Both a little shy, bookish, awkwardly unmarried in our early forties, and he'd made me laugh. We enjoyed the same restaurants, the same dumb movies and doing absolutely nothing on Sunday afternoons.

Besides, Skip hadn't minded my appearance. On first glance, most people usually notice something's not quite right, but they have trouble identifying what disturbs them. In a world where symmetry is the objective measure of beauty, I don't qualify. I was born with a cleft lip and a cleft palate.

My parents threw everything they had at fixing me. Eleven surgeries across eighteen years plus headgear and braces as a teenager, and the result is a slightly crooked nose, a tiny scar on my upper lip, a quirky lopsided smile, and a history of head colds that always turn straight into ear infections. But I can chew, breathe through my nose and speak clearly, which is pretty good, considering.

And Skip hadn't cared one whit. The first man I'd met who really, truly evaluated women—all people, for that matter—from the inside out.

I groaned. My litany sounded like a cheesy personal ad. But even my mother approved of Skip, although she'd been so desperate to get me married that her standards might have slipped some. His wealth—even though it came from such a proletarian source as car wash franchises—more than made up for his family's social deficiencies in her eyes. I was just happy to have finally found a companion I really liked, and who liked me back.

I slid my wedding ring past my knuckle then let it drop back into place. For better or for worse. In sickness and health. Till death—

My phone rang. Clarice spewed information. I scrambled to take legible notes.

"Call me when you get there," she finished. "I'll be on the road in an hour."

I unlatched my seatbelt and stumbled up the aisle. The air steward was stretched out on a padded bench at the far end of the galley, his ankles crossed and an open Sudoku booklet covering his face.

I nudged his leg. "I need to change the destination."

~oOo~

Rain. Gray streaks on the jet's thick Plexiglas windows. I shivered. It was like waking up in a different world. I rubbed my dry, stinging eyes as the terminal slid by outside.

PDX—Portland International Airport. The fringe of civilization, at least compared to the heat and bustle of Cozumel and home in San Francisco.

Skip and I had planned that I would move into his loft after the honeymoon. My townhouse would be absorbed into his many property holdings. His eyes had lightened when he'd talked about navigating this new world for me. I know it sounds crazy, but his eyes always reminded me of butter rum Life Savers—a warm, golden brown. We'd be the intrepid pair.

No matter what he may or may not have done, I missed him. He'd been a reassuring presence, the same steady routine, the person I was always going to come home to. Until now.

I hoped he wasn't suffering. Would they kill him fast? Was he already dead? Had he planned his own abduction?

The plane lurched to a stop, and the fans and motors that had been white noise powered down. My ears popped when the steward opened the latch on the door.

"Do you have a jacket in easy reach in your luggage?" he asked.

"Probably," I mumbled.

"Take this." He handed me a blue windbreaker with the charter company's logo discretely printed on the chest pocket. "We hope to see you again soon."

I shrugged my arms into the sleeves and pulled up the hood. "Thanks." I clattered down the stairs and trotted toward the covered breezeway where my luggage waited piled on a cart.

Clarice had reserved a Chevy Tahoe for me at the Hertz desk. How much luggage did she think I had? I tossed the suitcases in the back, getting drenched in the process.

I hopped into the driver's seat and set the heater to full blast. I poked buttons until I had the windshield wipers going and the GPS system speaking in an annoying female monotone. I tapped in the address Clarice had given me.

I-205 north, across the Glenn L. Jackson Memorial Bridge into the Evergreen State. I'd never been to Washington before.

CHAPTER 4

The GPS woman kept insisting I turn where there wasn't a driveway. The checkered flag destination marker on the screen hovered in a blank area I assumed to be the solid acres of towering fir trees to my left. They looked exactly like the forest crowding in on my right. After my fourth three-point turn on the narrow two-lane road—no risk of oncoming traffic out here—I pulled onto the gravel shoulder and punched the mute button. The way things were going, I'd be sleeping in the vehicle that night. Maybe having a Tahoe would come in handy after all.

My phone rang—a restricted number.

My heart lurched. Maybe it was Skip's kidnappers with a ransom demand. "Hello?" My hand was shaking so much I could hardly hold the phone to my ear.

Heavy breathing, and it wasn't mine.

"Just let me talk to him," I begged. "Whatever you want, I'll get it for you."

"Nora? It's Robbie." His voice was froggy. He's a smart kid, but he always looked as though he'd slept in his clothes. How does someone endure the rigors of Stanford summa cum laude and still maintain the pudginess and innocent, geeky sweetness of a barely pubescent boy?

"Where are you?" I asked.

"I—um—I can't say."

"Don't be ridiculous. Has the FBI been in to the office yet?"

"They don't need to."

"Robbie." I tried to keep my tone level and measured even though I wanted to scream at him. "This is very important. Skip's in danger. His life depends upon it.

I need you to go into the office and secure the company's financial records. I need—"

"It's too late. I know, all right?" Robbie burst in. "I've been feeding them information. I've been talking to them for almost a year now. I'm really sorry, all right? But they had some—well, some information—about me—I can't—" He panted into the phone. "I just found out about Skip. I can't believe it. They never said there'd be a physical threat. Never. I gotta go. I'm sorry, Nora."

"Wait!" I yelled. "Who? Who have you been talking to?"

"Everyone. All the clients, of course, then the FBI. They promised."

I had a stranglehold on the steering wheel. "What did they promise?"

But Robbie was gone.

Slowly, the rain's drumming on the roof replaced the pounding in my ears. The headlight beams illuminated water droplets like sparkles—the rapid shimmy of wet tinsel. I pitched forward and rested my head on the airbag cover.

I couldn't even think. Where my ideas should be— the rush of problems and solutions that ought to be matching up with each other—was dark, a deep void. Nothing. Nothing.

I jolted upright at a knuckle rapping on my window. The wavy shadow of a person appeared through the rain-rippled glass. I pressed the button to lower the window a few inches.

"Mrs. Sheldon?" Water dripped off the tip of his nose.

How was it that lately strange men knew my name?

"Someone named Clarice called and said I should be out looking for you."

"God bless that woman," I muttered.

"I don't think He'd approve of the language she uses."

I grinned. "Probably not."

"If you'll turn around and follow me, I'll show you up to the main house."

"You've got yourself a deal. And thanks."

He hunkered back into the collar of his jacket and stumped through the puddles to his truck.

I stuck close to his taillights. He pulled off the road into an indentation in the shrubbery, a spot just wide enough for his truck between two trees. He sat idling for a minute then his pickup lurched forward, and I saw what we'd been waiting for—a motorized gate, nearly overgrown with ivy. The rain had parted gaps in the leaves, revealing glimpses of a wrought iron structure underneath. No keypad, so it must have a motion sensor. The only way I'd have ever found it was by whacking the bushes with a stick along this stretch of empty county road. Good grief.

Clarice's reason for the Chevy Tahoe became apparent the first time my head hit the roof even though I still had my seatbelt buckled. There was a horrible, grating crunch as an axle dug a trough through what felt like a sandbar littered with fist-sized rocks. I punched the 4-Lo button, and the engine ground lower, into a deep slogging sound. I was going to have nice purple bruises across my hips and left shoulder in the morning.

Fortunately, my chaperone seemed to think a leisurely pace was a good idea. I followed his lead, gunning and braking over a track that would surely qualify for those crazy off-road motorcycle races on ESPN—the ones I skip over on my way to more interesting shows. I should have been paying attention.

Then the truck in front of me went vertical, and I got a really good look at his rusty tailgate. The pickup bucked, flung mud onto my windshield from its rear wheels, then roared up and over what I now realized was the side of a gully—a gully I was still in. Oh boy.

I sucked a deep breath, clenched my teeth and punched the accelerator. My stomach flipped a few loops when terra firma disappeared from view. That's when I scrunched my eyes closed, forgot to keep my jaw closed, bit my tongue, and landed upright, bouncing hard on the Tahoe's shocks but clear of the gully.

After that it was just big rocks and crater-sized potholes—in other words, clear sailing. And the clouds decided to open up in earnest, proving the earlier downpour just a warm-up session. The windshield wipers were useless.

The pickup's taillights doubled bright as the driver hit the brakes. I did the same. A minute later, my door was wrenched open.

"Not likely to let up," he huffed. "Leave what you don't need for later. Ready?"

I grabbed my purse and slid off the seat. My sandals were no match for the tangled, sopping, calf-high grass. I stumbled after my rescuer, trying to yank the windbreaker hood up at the same time.

He pulled open a wood door, its peeling paint curling up in long strips. We tumbled into a dingy, echoing room with scuffed linoleum tiles in alternating turquoise and beige.

He pulled off his hat and slapped it against his leg, releasing an arc of water droplets. "You can shelter here for now. I brought you some dinner." He jerked a thumb toward a massive table in the center of the room, on which sat a plate covered with aluminum foil. "I'll be back later to help unload and show you around. Don't like to leave the boys when it's storming like this." He set a hand on the door's crash bar.

"Wait," I blurted. "Your name?"

"Walt. Walt Neftali. Caretaker, of sorts. Mostly I run the boys' camp and try to keep vagrants and squatters from destroying what's left of the property."

"This is the main house?"

He nodded. "Kitchen. There's more—" He gestured toward the dark end of the room, away from the windows. "But the electrical wiring is ancient and currently on the fritz, so you'd need a flashlight. Sorry about no heat. If I'd known you were coming—" His forehead wrinkled into horizontal ridges. "Well, I don't know what I'd have done different. Been so long since any of the chimneys have been cleaned that the place would probably burn down if I started a fire. Place is about to fall down as it is. But—" He shrugged. "Welcome."

"Thank you." It came out like a whimper.

Walt nodded once more, tugged the knit hat back on his head, and left me alone.

~oOo~

The rain continued through the night, and Walt did not return. Not that I expected him to. I'm a grown woman, and I can take care of myself.

Besides it sounded as though Walt had his hands full with a group of boys. No matter their number or ages, I'd definitely be out of my league dealing with a bunch of bored, cooped-up boys. While Walt seemed like a capable

23

man, I wasn't going to begrudge him the time he needed to care for his charges.

Dinner turned out to be two ham slices, a spoonful of baked beans, a mound of coleslaw, and a pineapple ring. I devoured it so fast I didn't even taste it.

The cell phone signal waffled between half and one bar, but I was able to leave a short message for Clarice.

When it became clear I'd need to make the kitchen into my sleeping quarters for the night, I cinched up the windbreaker, dashed out to the Tahoe, grabbed the first two suitcases my hands landed on and trudged them back to the dim kitchen. Thunder rippled overhead, ending in an earsplitting crack as another flash of lightning took the first one's place.

Squinting through the gloom and working more by feel than sight, I unzipped the suitcases, pulled out anything soft, and formed a nest on the tabletop. With the house empty and neglected for as long as Walt had hinted at, there was a possibility rats or other undesirable creatures might become my bunkmates. There was no way I was going to stretch out on the floor, and I was trying really hard not to think about those animals having the kind of feet and toes that enabled them to climb table legs fast and silently.

I fell asleep curled around a pile of Skip's soft T-shirts.

CHAPTER 5

A blaring horn tore through my subconscious. I sat up fast, clutched the edge of the wobbly table and squeezed my eyes shut against the sunlight streaming through the dirty windows. I groaned and took another quick peek. Nothing had changed since last night.

Except the horn, which was now being punctuated into shorter and longer blasts. Made me wonder if it was Morse code. I never was a Girl Scout or Brownie or member of whatever youth league you learn that sort of skill in, so the meaning was lost on me.

I rolled off the table and staggered to the door. I pushed it open far enough to get a welcome glimpse of a silver Subaru station wagon with California plates. And stooped in the open driver's door, punching the horn, was a stout, wrinkled woman with the biggest mushroom-colored bouffant I have ever seen.

Clarice is indispensable to me. I'd brought her with me from my last job when I started at the foundation. Twice widowed and childless, she'd essentially adopted me as her own personal project, and I would never have developed so much professionally—or personally—without her. If I'd lived in pre-war England, she would have filled the role of a spinster great-aunt—the surrogate nanny who ruled with an iron glare, stayed on well past when her job was completed, and who would take my side against all adversity. In this day and age, she was the fixer on my staff and my most honest friend. Who needs a pet bulldog when you have Clarice?

"Nora," Clarice hollered. "You're in there? Good heavens. If you had any sense, you'd have slept in the

Tahoe last night. If I'd known this place was so rundown, I'd have sent you to the chalet in Aspen."

"It's not so bad." I stepped out onto the cracked concrete of what used to be a patio and yawned. "There's a chalet in Aspen?"

"Among others." Clarice waved a paper in the air. "I compiled a list of Skip's private properties."

"How about coffee?"

"Yes, please. I've been driving all night."

My shoulders slumped. "I'm sorry. I meant, did you bring some? There's definitely no coffee here." I ran a hand through my tangled hair. "All night? You just got here?" Boy, it was taking me a while to catch up. "Thank you."

"Here, lady." Something nudged my thigh.

I jumped and glanced down into clear sea-blue eyes in a small face that was more freckle than not.

"Mr. Walt says he's sorry he didn't come back last night. We got a leak." A nervous tick, like a half-wink, interrupted his train of thought. He sniffed and bumped the edge of the paper plate against my leg again. "Here's your breakfast."

"Thank you." I knelt beside him and gave him my best smile. "You live here?"

The boy nodded then tipped his head toward Clarice. "Who's she?"

"My friend."

"She's crabby."

I chuckled and whispered. "And she's always like that. It never gets better."

The boy's eyes widened.

"Oh, phoo," Clarice huffed, walking up to us. "I'm a grouch until I've had coffee, then I'm sweet as pie." She hacked the terrible smoker's cough she still had.

"We're not allowed coffee. Only Mr. Walt, but he didn't have time this morning," the boy said.

"Course not," Clarice announced. "The caffeine would stunt your growth." She leaned down until her face was inches from the boy's. "And we wouldn't want that now, would we?"

I grabbed the plate from the boy's shaking hands. "Please thank Mr. Walt for me."

The boy stood, transfixed, staring at Clarice. Her face is like a roadmap of Canyon Country covered with half an inch of pancake foundation. It had survived an all-night drive without fissure. I could understand the boy's fascination.

"There a town around here?" Clarice barked.

The boy flinched, then pointed. "That way. We go twice a month for supplies."

I gently squeezed his shoulder. "Thank you. You can go now."

He glanced at me, and I nodded encouragingly. He disappeared as silently as he'd come.

"You scared him." I frowned at Clarice.

"Huh." Clarice raised the paper towel with a gnarled but perfectly manicured fingertip and glared at the plate's contents. "Refined carbohydrates and saturated fat. We gotta find a grocery store."

I stuffed the better part of a cinnamon roll—the kind that comes in a pressurized cardboard tube—in my mouth and mumbled around it. "Now?"

"You got something better to do?" Clarice replied over her shoulder as she marched back to her car. "Get in."

The return trip to the paved road was much easier when it wasn't pouring buckets. Clarice navigated around boulders and inexplicable pits with amazing dexterity. It was as though one of the boys' camp activities had been handing each child a shovel and giving them the go-ahead to dig to China.

A few blue patches appeared between floaty clouds that no longer had heavy underbellies. I kept my mouth packed with sausage links and additional cinnamon roll in order to protect against the teeth-jarring I'd experienced the previous night. Besides, the rutted track required all of Clarice's concentration and was not conducive to conversation.

Clarice pulled through the automatic gate onto the county road. Steam rose off the pavement in wispy waves.

I swallowed and cleared my throat. "I heard from Robbie."

She shot me an arched-brow glance and stomped on the accelerator.

"He's been informing the FBI—of what, I don't know—for a year. It sounded like he was on the run. Again, I don't know why."

Clarice turned toward me, her drawn-on brows flattened in a fierce line above her narrowed eyes. "That weasel."

"Well, I don't know. If there was something illegal going on, he had to—"

A flash of mangy brown fur and antlers crossed the windshield.

I screamed.

Clarice stomped on the brakes, and we both slammed against our seatbelts.

The animal—like a deer, but bigger, with its neck stretched uncomfortably by the weight of its antlers—stood straddling the yellow line and slowly turned its head our way. It blinked in a leisurely fashion, its nostrils flaring.

"What is that?" I breathed.

"Stupid—" Clarice rasped, "—elk, I presume, never having seen one in person before. Stupid!" she yelled and cranked down her window. "Shoo. Shoo." She flapped her arm out the window.

The elk was unimpressed—and unmoved.

Clarice honked, long and loud.

The elk took a step toward us, its head lowered.

"You're scaring it." I patted Clarice's shoulder, then squeezed as the elk swung its head in a menacing gesture.

With a terrific charge, the elk nailed the grille with its rack. The station wagon rocked back on its heels, jouncing us in our seats. The elk backed up, shuffling his feet for another attack.

Clarice pulled her arm in and rolled up the window. "Scared? I don't think so." She revved the gas pedal.

"Oh, no. No, no, no. You are not taking on the wildlife." I clutched the dashboard.

"Evasive maneuvers, girl. He'll never know what swept right past him." She let the car roll forward then jerked the wheel hard to the right. The tires spit gravel and balked for a second before we got traction and shot down the shoulder and bounced back up onto the pavement.

I twisted and glanced out the rear window. The elk was still standing in the middle of the road, ready to challenge the next car to intrude on his territory. "You're making friends left and right this morning," I muttered.

"Low blood sugar," Clarice gritted between clenched teeth as she hunched over the steering wheel.

I closed my eyes against the blur of trees whirring by and concentrated on breathing. At the word *town*, I'd been anticipating a series of light-controlled intersections, several choices for grocery shopping, banks, a library, an ice cream shop. I'd even settle for strip malls populated with nail salons, questionable sushi bars, and laundromats. There had to be at least one drive-through espresso stand.

When the car rocked to a stop and I cracked my eyelids open, I saw trees—more trees. Actually, I saw the trunks. At least they weren't moving. I had to tilt way back to see to their tops. Their needled branches rippled like feathers in the stiff breeze.

"Come on," Clarice grunted and popped open her door.

A weather-beaten building with a covered porch along the front occupied one corner at a crossroads. The opposite corner boasted a dilapidated service station with a U.S. Post Office sign in the dirt-streaked front window. A teetering gingerbread Victorian house—probably technically a mansion when it was built, but no longer extravagant—spread her flanged porticoes in the third corner. The painted lady's trim had merged into worn shades of taupe. The fourth corner was filled with hip-high weeds.

"I'm guessing this is it," Clarice panted as she clumped up sagging steps next to a rusty ice cooler with a faded bait sign taped to the front.

"Maybe we should go a little farther. Maybe there's a Safeway."

"You want to be cooped up in the car with me for another hundred miles?" she growled.

We pushed through a glass door into a cramped, dim space. I bumped a display of Corn Nuts and Skoal chewing tobacco. Together—in one display. I was stuck for a second wrapping my head around that marketing concept.

Clarice grabbed my arm and propelled me past the chips, jerky, infant formula, and canned goods to the bank of buzzing coolers in the back. She pulled my forearms into a platform and loaded me up with eggs, half and half, frozen concentrated orange juice, and Canadian bacon. For such a small store, they had an amazing selection.

Clarice darted down an aisle and returned with a jar of instant coffee.

"But—"

"It'll do for now. We should have checked the cupboards before we left. Any idea if there's a coffee maker? Frying pan?"

I shook my head dumbly.

"Toilet paper," Clarice muttered, and disappeared again.

I stood patiently while my personal shopper scoped out the store, ticking through her be-ready-for-any-emergency mental checklist. I slowly rotated, taking in the hand-lettered signs advertising specials with prices I hadn't seen in San Francisco in years, the crates full of gigantic, fresh from the orchard, unwaxed and unstickered apples in the far corner, the fat calico cat that ambled out from behind the as yet unattended cashier's counter. Who lived in a town like this? The floor squeaked under my weight as I shifted.

A pair of sharp dark eyes—and a lean, swarthy man stepped out from behind an endcap display of Rainier beer. He stared straight at me, his smooth cheeks unflinching, taut body, shiny brass belt buckle the size of a salad plate, uplifted chin, perfect line of a black mustache. Mexican, he had to be.

And suddenly I knew—they'd sent an emissary, someone to negotiate Skip's release. Maybe someone who'd been there, on the beach, someone who knew.

My arms went numb, the groceries weighing on them, and blood surged in my ears and throat. I opened my mouth but nothing came out.

The man's gaze changed from frank appraisal to a concerned scowl, then he looked down—to a little girl in a pink tutu and Hello Kitty sweater tugging on his jeans. She held a bag of Skittles in her open palm with a wordless plea in her eyes. He smiled at her and nodded.

The instant grin of delight on her face brought my breath back. I sagged against a cooler door. Just a father and his daughter. Just doing what I was doing—grocery shopping. I panted like a marathon runner.

"Miss?" He was at my elbow.

"I'm okay," I whispered.

He held my gaze long enough to let me know he didn't believe me. Then he grasped his little girl's hand and led her to the counter.

"What was that about?" Clarice layered a couple more items on me.

"Felt like a panic attack. Which I've never had before. For a second I thought—I thought he might know about Skip—might be able to tell me—" I inhaled shakily.

"Nonsense. We're in the middle of nowhere, which is exactly why I picked this place. No way they could get here that fast. Besides, panic attacks are for sissies. Get angry. It's easier and more productive." Clarice pushed me toward the checkout counter. "I know what I'm talking about."

The man and his daughter were gone. I'd heard a bell clank while Clarice was lecturing me and realized it was the signal attached to the front door in the form of a cluster of small cowbells dangling from the handle. A beat-up blue pickup eased out of the parking lot and through the intersection after a rolling stop. I just caught the top of the little girl's head and a dash of pink tulle in the passenger seat.

"Mornin'." The flannel-clad woman behind the cash register nodded a greeting, then slanted a second look at Clarice.

Due to my facial asymmetry, I'm accustomed to receiving short, awkwardly polite stares, but Clarice usually gets the full head-swivel double take. I suppose it's not every day a Margaret Thatcher lookalike shows up at an American place of business, especially now that Margaret Thatcher is dead. Having Clarice around is a kind of guilty blessing because she takes the attention off me. I dumped our groceries on the counter.

I dug through my purse and pulled out my wallet while the woman rang up the items by punching keys—no barcode scanner here. I flipped through my credit card selection, trying to decide which one to use. I carried a couple company cards and one foundation-issued card, but I still had my personal Bank of America Visa which I slapped on the glass-topped counter over the slide-out tray of scratch-off tickets.

The woman looked distinctly uncomfortable. The corner of her mouth twitched. "We don't take plastic. Just cash. Or a check if it's not out of state."

"Oh." I darted a glance at Clarice who was also shocked into open-mouthed silence—a rare occurrence.

We both dove back into our purses, hunting for the green stuff. We came up with a few crumpled bills but nowhere near enough.

"Looks like you're buying necessities," the woman said.

"Up the road about twenty minutes." I pointed, as if that was helpful. "Walt—um, Walt Neftali works there, and there's a boys' camp."

"Oh, you're staying at the poor farm. Hope they came through the storm last night okay. I'll start an account for you. Name?"

I provided the details and signed her form. "When do I pay?" I stretched to the side and snagged a few packages of cookies off a nearby display. I shoved them into the grocery lineup still waiting to be tallied, pretending I didn't see Clarice's scowl.

"End of the month, or thereabouts. I'm Etherea Titus, by the way. Own this place with my husband, Bob. Pleased to meetcha." She wrote our total on the account form and shoved four bulging paper sacks across the counter.

Back in the car, it took me a few minutes of flying trees and dashed yellow line whizzing under the fender so fast it appeared solid to gather my thoughts. "Do you want to talk about this?"

"No." Clarice polished off the last of a banana and stuffed the peel in the cup holder in the Subaru's console.

"My husband of short duration is missing. He may or may not be alive. He may or may not be on the FBI's most wanted list. I'm waiting for a phone call demanding ransom. My current residence is a poor farm." I ticked each problem on my fingers. "I don't know how much longer I'll have the right to stay there—and then what? I may or may not have access to any money. I hope Etherea isn't disappointed at the end of the month, but I'd pay my last penny just to get some answers." I bit my lip at the reemergence of a thought that had been nagging me, and I turned toward Clarice. "What if I'm under suspicion too?"

Clarice tore open a Clif bar while steering with her knee. "You're right. It can't possibly get worse. But you've got me. That counts on the plus side." She swerved back into the right lane and stuffed the end of the energy bar in her mouth.

From the depths of my purse, my phone rang. Heartbeat in overdrive, I bent in half and rummaged until I snagged the phone.

I groaned when I saw the caller ID. "My mother."

"What?" Clarice screeched. "For all she knows you're still on your honeymoon. You didn't call her, did you?" She grabbed the phone and tossed it over her shoulder into the backseat. "You have enough problems."

"What if it's about Dad?" I stretched my arm between the seats.

"Stop." Clarice smacked my leg. "Listen to the message later. Then decide if you should call her back."

I sighed. She was right. Describing my mother as high-maintenance would be a compliment compared to some of the other things I could say. And if Dad had had another episode, it was too late already.

"The way I see it—on all those points you listed— we're waiting. I don't know what you could do to make anything better. Agreed?" Clarice shoved the wrapper next to the banana peel and daintily wiped the corners of her mouth of any errant lipstick.

I pressed my fingertips to my forehead. "So we're camping—indefinitely."

"Might not be so bad. I picked the remotest of Skip's properties. No one will bother us. We'll get the call. And in the meantime you'll do what you can to keep the car wash business running." She slowed and pulled into the indentation to our secret gate.

I peered hard at the sentry trees. I was going to have to establish landmarks in my mind, or I wouldn't be able to make a grocery run by myself. Self-sufficiency was suddenly of the utmost importance.

"I forgot." Clarice pointed a burgundy-tipped finger at the glove compartment. "I brought one of those wi-fi hot spot thingies. We'll be connected, even if we are in the boonies."

We bounced through the gully, and a few of the larger rocks were starting to look familiar. I wondered how hard it would be to get a road grader out here. Probably would need a backhoe first.

The main house came into sight, as did a navy blue sedan parked next to my Tahoe. It was the kind that police use—a big, beefy thing with black wheel rims and a push bar bolted to the front bumper. It had U.S. Government license plates.

"You know what I said about things not getting worse?" Clarice muttered. "I take that back."

CHAPTER 6

Clarice guided the Subaru in a slow roll past the government sedan. "Empty," she rasped in her lowest tone which is several decibels above a stage whisper.

We were both slouched in our seats gangster-style, straining to see out the Subaru's windows and through the government sedan's tinted windows without appearing as though we cared in the least.

"Which means he's already searching the place," she continued. "Should we make a run for it?"

"Why delay the inevitable? I need coffee."

Clarice parked, and I scooted out of the station wagon, hauling a grocery sack with me. Just as I reached the kitchen door, it swung open.

A tall, broad-shouldered man filled the opening. He held a screwdriver in one hand and a pair of pliers in the other. Big hands. He held the tools as though he knew what to do with them. As though they had weapon capabilities.

I jumped back.

Clarice let out a grunt when I landed on her foot.

I dropped the sack and grabbed her arm. My toes dug in for a track start, muscles poised to launch into a full sprint.

"Wait! Wait." The man held his arms wide as if to prove he was harmless. "It's not what you think."

"You wanna know what I think?" Clarice growled.

A short smile flitted across his face. "Um, no." He tucked the tools in the back pockets of his jeans and returned his hands where we could see them. "I'm Matt Jarvis. Noticed your power was out. Checked your breakers and the grounding on a few of these old outlets. You'll be safe to plug in small appliances now."

"Coffee?" My voice came out squeaky.

His hazel-eyed gaze took a long time, traveling from the top of my head all the way down to my feet and back up to my face. He didn't stop and leer at any particular spots, though, didn't seem to notice my lip scar. He gave a curt nod and turned.

"Well, well, well," Clarice muttered. "Our tax dollars at work."

"Be nice," I whispered as I knelt beside her to collect the stray groceries.

"I doubt this is a social call. We need to get you a lawyer."

"Freddy?" The contents of the paper sack bulged behind a few growing holes. I clasped it against my chest.

"Might as well." Clarice balanced a couple tuna cans under my chin. "Go entertain our gentleman caller, and I'll see if I can wake the dead."

The pungent, comforting scent of freshly ground coffee beans filled the kitchen. Matt tipped a small electric grinder and dumped the grounds into a stainless steel French press.

"At least the kitchen is well-equipped." I nodded toward the French press.

"It's mine," Matt said. "Part of my emergency kit. How'd you sleep?" He glanced pointedly at the tabletop nest of rumpled clothing that still bore my body-shaped hollow.

I scowled. "Fine." I pushed a corner clear and started unloading the sack.

"That was a sneaky move—the flight plan change while en route. A few of my superiors aren't very happy with you. They pulled me off vacation to be your welcoming committee, so I'm not very happy either."

I thunked a can of chili on the table. "You want me to be sorry? My husband is missing. He might even be dead. I'm waiting for a ransom phone call. On a misery scale—from one to ten—I think I win." I jabbed my hand back in the sack. Something thin and hard scraped my fingers and jammed under my wedding ring. I sucked in a sharp breath and pulled out the can opener stuck to my hand like a blood-sucking leech. I turned my back to Matt and pressed my hand into my stomach, trying to pry the tool loose.

"Let me see." Matt cleared a bigger space on the corner of the table. "Sit." He pushed me back until I bumped the edge and scooted up onto the tabletop.

My finger was already red and swelling against the constraint of the ring plus the can opener handle. I scrunched my eyes closed against the pain. If the ring hadn't been too big in the first place, this wouldn't have happened.

The kettle on the stove warbled a faint whistle.

Matt pressed my wrist against my thigh, and I groaned.

"Don't look," he said as he rustled through the paper sack. Then he started rubbing something cool and slimy on my finger, massaging it into the spaces around my ring. The kettle's whistle escalated to a scream. Then a yank, and the can opener came free.

My eyes flew open, and I peeked down—at my hand smeared with minty fresh blue gel. "Toothpaste?"

Matt grinned, and I found myself grinning back into those hazel eyes.

"It was handy." He dropped my wedding ring in my right palm and moved across the room to snap off the gas burner.

"Which agency are you with?" I cranked the kitchen faucet and rubbed my hands under the stream of frigid water.

"FBI." He must have heard my groan as he pulled a couple mugs from a cupboard and blew dust out of them. "You have a problem with that?"

"I was hoping for a little variety. CIA. IRS. Why not make it a party?" I balanced my ring on the windowsill above the sink then grabbed one of Skip's T-shirts and dried my hands on it.

"I don't think you realize what kind of trouble you're in." Matt was suddenly close—very close, and staring hard into my eyes. It was a principal's-office glare, intimidating and nothing romantic about it, but I flushed like a giddy schoolgirl. Heat zipped straight up my neck to the roots of my hair in nothing flat.

"I didn't do anything," I breathed.

"We'll leave that for the grand jury. But prison would be pleasant compared to what might happen if any of your husband's associates assume you have information they want. You know Felix Gonzalo Ochoa?"

I shook my head.

"Ziggy Beltran? Martin Zimmermann, also known as Mart the Shark? Fat Al Canterino?"

My head hurt, I was shaking it so hard.

"Well, you don't want to. Part of my job is to make sure any contact these guys might have with you is civil." Matt pulled the damp T-shirt out of my clenched fist and replaced it with a mug of coffee.

"Witness protection?" I whispered.

"What have you witnessed?" At my blank look, Matt continued, "Nope. I need the contact info for all of your husband's relatives."

"Good luck with that." Clarice snorted from the doorway. "He was essentially a foundling. A flaky biological mother who never took responsibility for him, and that's it."

I frowned at her. It wasn't Skip's fault he got a rough start in life. Part of what drove him so hard to succeed was the desire to prove he wasn't tied to his roots. "I do have his mother's phone number. Skip told her about the wedding, but she chose not to attend."

The kitchen door creaked open again behind Clarice. She reached back and slammed it shut. "Everything around here's falling apart. Figures," she huffed and thumped her purse—the size of a toaster oven—on the table. She pulled out her bulging, old-school Day-Timer. "Loretta was probably so sloshed she couldn't stand up on the big day. Her no-show has nothing to do with you."

Clarice's impression of my mother-in-law was obtained from one brief meeting. Loretta had visited the foundation office one day while I was on a trip to review an orphanage in Argentina. According to Clarice, she was mostly incoherent and mumbling and reeked of alcohol. She'd made obvious efforts with her clothing and makeup but was in no condition to drive and had to be escorted into a taxi. She'd given her address as a Holiday Inn Express in Alameda Point.

I know Skip supports his mother. I've seen the checks—it's not a secret. But I don't think he wants us to become best friends.

"Let me call her—please?" I reached for the note Clarice had scribbled from her Day-Timer and glanced at

Matt. "There's no way she'd be able to pay a ransom, so I'll just tell her to call me if she hears anything."

Matt didn't look happy about my request, but he gave a brief nod after a moment's hesitation.

Clarice helped herself to a mug of coffee while I dialed. I bit my lip, listening to the ringing on Loretta's end. I was on the verge of panic about having to leave a message when a faint "Hello?" sounded.

"Loretta?" I gulped a quick breath. "It's Nora. Nora Ingram, uh, Sheldon." Saying my new last name still felt awkward.

"Darling, how are you? Is Skip behaving? I miss him."

"Um—" I bent over the phone and squeezed my eyes shut.

"Oh, I know he is," Loretta continued. She sounded surprisingly light and articulate. "My best boy. Do you know what he did? He found this nice place for me to stay. Of course I can't have a drink here, not even one tiny sip, but the food is fabulous, and the staff is amazing. They come and tell me when it's time for the next activity. No chance to rest. Group therapy sessions, tai chi, spa treatments from sunup to sundown."

"Where are you?" I asked.

"Something Springs. Crystal Springs? Certainty Springs? Or maybe Serendipity Solstice...Sunrise Something. Oh dear," Loretta sighed. "I'm terrible at names. Wait. It's embroidered on my robe." Soft fumbling came through the line, then she said, "Serenity Springs Spa. Three S's. I should remember that."

It sounded like a high-end detox place. The word *spa* is commonly a Californian euphemism for a rehab facility.

"Darling? I have to go. Andre is waving at me. It's time for my paraffin dip. Call again, okay, honey?" Loretta hung up.

I balanced the phone in my palm and sagged against the edge of the table.

"You didn't tell her," Matt blurted, his jaw clenched.

"She sounded happy. And she didn't ask—she just assumed—" I shook my head. "I don't have the heart to worry her until I know for sure. Is there a chance Skip hid her in a safe place before—before this incident?" My voice trailed into a whisper. "Was he planning this?"

Matt's eyes narrowed. "Where is she?"

I gave him the name of the spa. "If she's safe, let's just leave her alone. Maybe it'll work this time."

"This time?" Matt took the paper with Loretta's number on it and made a few notes.

"Four, by my count," Clarice said. "Every six months or so. She usually lasts about ten days, but her record in one treatment center is two months."

"So we have time," I added. "Please?" I touched Matt's sleeve. "Maybe we can figure things out, find Skip, and she doesn't have to know. She's so fragile, and he's all she has."

Matt stared hard at me again, searching for something. What did he want to see? I glanced away.

He inhaled deeply. "We *will* figure it out. But finding your husband?" He raised my chin with his index finger, forcing eye-contact. "Don't hold your breath. You won't find much on Google about those men I mentioned, but what is there is interesting reading." He dropped a business card on the table beside me. "I'll be back."

CHAPTER 7

Clarice and I waited in silence until the sound of Matt's big-engined sedan crunching over the rutted tracks faded.

"Good for us he forgot his French press." Clarice refilled her mug. "Why are there no chairs in here?" She propped one padded hip against the counter and scowled around the kitchen. Fuchsia lipstick prints ringed her mug.

I pinched the bridge of my nose against a stabbing pain that seemed to be splitting my forehead. "Freddy?"

"Voice mail. I left three messages for good measure. Also tried Leroy and got his wife. He went out yesterday afternoon and hasn't come home yet. Sounds like behavior she's accustomed to. Feels fishy to me."

Clarice heaved a sigh and scooped my hiking boots off the floor. I'd rejected them last night as being too hard to sleep with. She shoved them against my chest. "I'm sticking, no matter what. You know that. But you need to get thinking, girl. Get us out of this mess. Go on." She gave me a push toward the door. "I'll rustle up some level of domesticity while you're pondering."

I'm a rambler, as Clarice well knows. I've worn a groove in the sidewalks of Nob Hill and along the piers. I plopped down on the stoop outside and traded my sandals for the boots. Just tying the laces is therapeutic for me.

I jumped up and dashed through the door again.

Clarice was already folding clothes and tidying the mess on the tabletop. "Forget this?" She held out my think-things-through notebook and mechanical pencil, my tools of the trade.

"And this." I enveloped her in a monster squeeze. "What would I ever do without you?"

"Oooof." Clarice pushed me away and sniffed. "Go on."

Shhnork grumpf shnuff bump—from under the table.

Clarice and I stared at each other wide-eyed.

I backed away and peered under the table.

Two beady eyes buried in deep, fleshy wrinkles glinted back. The delicate edges of its snout rippled with eager inquisitiveness as its neck stretched forward.

I giggled.

"What?" Clarice bent over just as the pig emerged. "Aaaiee. Get it away from me." She flailed a few karate chops in the air and staggered backward, crashing into a pie safe. "What is that?" She slapped a hand over her heaving bosom.

The potbellied pig followed in her wake, snorting greedily.

I could hardly breathe for laughing. The pig had a collar, so I grabbed it and dragged the little porker away from its active investigation of Clarice's taupe Naturalizer loafers. Its hoofed feet skidded, splayed on the linoleum tiles.

"You're a wildlife magnet," I chuckled. "It must have followed you in earlier."

"Bah." Clarice scowled at the pig.

The pig scrutinized her right back, its mouth open in a lolling guffaw expression as though it had just heard a raunchy joke. It was mostly pink with a few black blotches. One blotch covered its left eye in a half mask like a rakish Lone Ranger.

I scratched it behind the ears, and it grunted accordingly. "See? Friendly."

"Out," Clarice announced, her rigid arm pointing in an emphatic, no-nonsense gesture. "Pigs live outside. Take it with you." She muttered a few other things I won't repeat, and I lured the pig to safety with a stale bit of leftover cinnamon roll.

I knelt beside the pig, and it shnuffled my fingers for crumbs.

"Who do you live with? You don't look neglected."

It blinked.

I patted the side of its round belly and pushed off my haunches. "Want to give me the tour?"

The pig took off trotting, its curly tail bobbing in time with its steady gait. I stuffed my notebook in the back pocket of my jeans and fell into line. Clean, cold air—I inhaled deeply and savored the ache in my lungs.

A bit of meadow surrounded the house. More like a mansion, really. Three stories of brick and crumbling, ivy-covered colonnades in the center with two-story wings off each end. The kitchen was in the back of one of these wings. Slate roof with moss grown thick in every crevice. If this had been a poor farm, I wondered how the wealthy had lived.

It was still thickly overcast, the clouds so low the roof's peaks sliced through them as they drifted overhead. I shivered and blew on my hands.

An impatient grunt drew my attention to the tree line where my escort waited beside a cud-chewing goat.

I squinted to make sure I wasn't hallucinating. What was with the random animals? I couldn't imagine the place was still functioning as a producing farm. A petting zoo?

The goat had stubby horns, so I gave it a wide berth even though it was tethered. No point in testing the length of that rope. I slipped between two enormous trees into a different world—tangled vines sprawled across the ground and climbed soaring trunks; flitting chatter turned out to be tiny birds scouring unseen insects from tree bark. Collected condensation dripped off branches onto the thick layer of dead pine needles at my feet in soft syncopated plops. Peaceful and eerie at the same time.

Rustling undergrowth told me which direction the pig was taking. It took a while and some stumbling about to find the narrowly trod path. The pig was following a trace, probably etched into its little brain through repetition. I caught a whiff of wood smoke.

I tripped over a root and slammed my palm against the rough bark of a tree to catch my balance. When I glanced back up, the same boy from earlier stood in front of me, nonchalantly tapping the butt end of a hatchet against the side of his leg.

His crystal-clear, endless blue eyes drew me in. "Hello," I ventured.

"Are you lost?" the boy asked.

"Quite possibly."

"Orville knows the way. To his slop bucket at any rate."

I nodded as if his statement made sense.

"Wilbur's around here too, but he's anti-social."

"Is Wilbur the goat?" I jerked a thumb over my shoulder.

"No." The boy's tone was scornful. "Orville and Wilbur are twins. You know—" He took a practice swing at the nearest trunk with the hatchet. "When pigs fly."

"Oh. Of course."

"The goat's Terminator 'cause he has a four-part bionic stomach."

What kind of child was this? He couldn't be more than seven or eight, tossing about such bizarre and yet strangely informed phrases. "What's your name?" I asked.

"Eli."

A sage and a prophet, and precocious. I grinned. "Where are you going?"

A loud crack arced through the air and bounced off the trees—either a large branch breaking free or something else—something that sounded a lot like a gunshot. The idea seared through my mind, and I ducked instinctively. Eli's face mirrored my own startled fear.

Then the soft skin around his jaw hardened and he grabbed my hand. He tugged me off the semi-path into the undergrowth. We plunged through waist-high ferns and blackberries.

Eli darted, twisting and turning and stringing me along, beating a surprisingly quiet retreat through the woods. I kept an arm up to protect my face from the taller branches he dodged under and tried to pace my breathing. He was a speedy kid for such short legs.

Eli was wearing mud-encrusted sneakers, but his stealth was better matched to leather moccasins. Clearly this was not the first time he'd practiced such evasive maneuvers. Why would he need to? But since he didn't want to stick around, neither did I.

The trees dissipated—separated from en masse to individual trunks, and the gloom lightened. Eli pulled up short at the edge of a clearing, his hand hot and damp in mine.

A sprawling building slumped in the thick grass as though it couldn't muster the energy to admit residents. It was mostly single story except in places where the roof dipped even lower. A man—Walt—was on the roof in one of the swayback segments, straddling the ridge line and nailing bright, luminescent cedar shakes over bald spots. The whole building was a rangy patchwork of variously aged parts. One of the three river rock chimneys puffed reluctant smoke wisps.

Walt caught sight of us and waved his hammer. I glanced down and squeezed—nothing.

Eli was gone—just gone. There wasn't even an indentation in the dewy grass where he'd been standing. How had he slipped away without my noticing? And why?

Walt was edging toward a ladder propped against the close end of the building. I hurried forward and leaned on the ladder's rails to steady it while he descended.

"Some storm last night," he said.

"Do they happen often?"

"Fair bit. Several times a winter. Come in." Walt tipped his head toward the door. "Meet the boys."

I had to duck to avoid the door mantle and step over a high threshold at the same time to enter the building.

"This was the cattle hands' bunkhouse back when several hundred head of beef ranged these hills. Dairy cows were kept separate, up by the main road. Pampered, they were." Walt chuckled and led the way down a dark, narrow hall.

The remains of breakfast smells lingered in the stagnant air, plus the added scent of boys.

This is hard to explain, but boys, especially when they're growing fast, have an odor all their own, and it's not pleasant—mostly acrid, newly formed sweat with top notes of rancid clothing and vestiges of negligent grooming. It doesn't seem to bother them. In fact, they seem to wallow in it. I've encountered this same scent in the boys' wings of orphanages the world over. Women

49

everywhere are eternally grateful that the males of their species do eventually grow out of it.

The hallway emptied into a large, low room—the one with the working fireplace. Neat rows and columns of student desk-and-chair combos corralled boys bent over their books. A few laptops were propped open, their screens flickering. I did a quick count—twenty-one desks, four empty—seventeen boys. I wondered which desk belonged to Eli and why he wasn't in it when everyone else appeared so industrious.

It was hard to tell from the shy and curious glances from under brows and long-hanging forelocks, but the boys appeared to range from about ten years old to older teens. A few had dark shadows forming on their upper lips.

"Online courses," Walt murmured near my ear. "We have a tutor come help with advanced math and literary criticism as needed, as well as ACT and SAT test prep."

"And this is—" I whispered, then bit my lip and tried again. "Is Skip involved with this?"

Walt nodded. "He pays our accounts—at the general store and for repairs and maintenance. We're here rent free."

"Why—" I hesitated, not wanting to ask the reasons for this unusual situation in front of the boys. I also wondered just how many people Skip was supporting. I wasn't surprised, but I would have wanted to be part of it—if I'd known.

"Coffee? I finally got some brewing." Walt applied gentle pressure on my elbow and ushered me through a different doorway into a kitchen. It wasn't fancy, but the appliances were meant for large-scale cooking. Walt pointed to a stool at the peninsula countertop and stepped over to a gurgling coffee pot. "If you're here in a couple weeks, maybe you'd like to judge the creative writing contest. The boys get tired of hearing critiques from me. Poetry, plays, short stories—their submissions will run the gamut."

I accepted a steaming mug. "That's amazing. I don't think they do that even in the best private schools anymore."

"Probably not." Walt settled onto a stool opposite me. "I'm old-fashioned. The boys need to learn to imagine life through other people's perspectives, even if the people are fictional. Develops compassion, sympathy, empathy, and leadership."

"Is that why they're here? Needing to learn those traits?"

"Their parents, if they have them, or case workers think so. More often than not I think it's the adults in their lives who need those traits. The boys tend to straighten out on their own when they don't have the pressure of living in the difficult circumstances they come from."

"So they're in the system?"

"Most are. It's hard to place boys in foster homes generally, and older boys especially. Foster families are usually well intentioned, but not often well equipped to handle boys' aggression, compulsion for adventure and a challenge, the need for meaningful work beyond book learning." He shrugged and fingered the handle on his mug. His nails were cut short, with dirt shadows embedded in the rough calluses surrounding them. "The list goes on." His gaze wandered to the window as though he'd forgotten I was there.

Walt's nose was sharp and thin, pointed in profile. It'd been a few days since he'd shaved, and his stubble glinted red-gold in the window's light. He had blue eyes too, but not with the same clarity as Eli's. Could have been caused by a lifetime of worry. Maybe they were related.

"Eli?" I asked.

A slow smile spread across Walt's face, raising his ears and squinting the corners of his eyes. But he didn't answer or return his attention to me.

"He's younger than the other boys. And not studying this morning."

Walt turned at this, amusement in his eyes. "He found you in the woods, didn't he?"

I nodded.

"I figure when he's finished learning all there is to know out there, he'll come in, sit down, and devour everything there is to learn in here." He chuckled softly, his lips not parting. "Could take a couple decades for that to happen, though."

Walt seemed ageless. He spoke with the wisdom of a patient man who'd experienced acres of sorrow, but he didn't look old. My age even—maybe. "Is he yours?"

"Eli? Blood relation? No." Walt's gaze shifted back to the window. "But he reminds me of me."

"You're alone here."

He waited so long to answer I wasn't sure he'd heard me. He shoved his stool back and stood, gesturing to my mug. "Refill?" When I nodded, he said, "Suits me."

His back was straight and cold as he stretched out a long arm to pour more coffee. I'd gotten too personal, too fast. I wondered how long it had been since he'd had more than a cursory conversation with a woman.

I tried a different tack. "Are hunters allowed on the property?"

Walt's flash frown surprised me, as well as the intensity of his glare. "You've seen one?" If I hadn't already witnessed his placidity, his tone would have scared me.

I shook my head. "No. Heard one, maybe—I'm not sure. Could've been a gunshot. It frightened both Eli and me."

Walt's jaw worked in a slight, tense chewing motion, reminding me of Terminator the goat as he settled back on his stool. "I'll increase my patrols." He studied me for a moment. "But there is something you should know. We have a hermit. He's practically a phantom, invisible. But every once in a while he makes an appearance. Name's Dwayne, and if you call him by his name, he'll answer. Just so you know."

I was beginning to wonder what made the window so attractive that Walt couldn't keep his eyes from drifting over to it—or through it. Then he murmured, "I think Eli's found him, where he lives. And I think he's been apprenticing under Dwayne. That boy disappears like vapor. I'm lucky he still shows up for meals."

I took a deep breath, held it, then plunged in. "I have something you need to know too—why I'm here." I gave him the big picture, the big unknowns. I tried to leave my personal speculation out of the account, just stick to facts. From the intensity of Walt's frown, I figured he could hypothesize as well as I could.

"You're expecting them to contact you, here?" he asked.

"I hope so. It would mean he's still alive."

"How long are you going to wait?"

"As long as it takes."

Walt did the jaw clenching thing again. "Are you going to find out why? Skip doesn't deserve this." He exhaled long and hard, took his mug to the sink and rinsed it out. "Only met him twice. But given his history, his rough childhood, he really understood what the boys need. Mostly time and space." Walt leaned against the sink and crossed his arms. "I'm having trouble putting the two together. The good and the alleged bad. You too, I expect." He stared.

The beam of his full attention was disconcerting. I preferred his fascination with the window.

"You need anything, you'll tell me?" he asked.

I half shrugged.

"Yes. You must. The boys will help too. They don't know their benefactor, but they're good workers. I'll send over a crew this afternoon to set up living quarters for you. Won't be fancy, but it'll do."

I left the bunkhouse with instructions to follow the muddy rutted track that started behind Walt's parked pickup. I was to take the right-hand path at the first fork and the left-hand path at the second. He assured me the track would eventually pass by the main house.

I also came away with a fierce determination to make sure Walt and the boys didn't suffer from Skip's absence. I needed to find out how they were being funded and ensure the support continued. Maybe in that process, I'd find clues about my other problems.

Follow the money. I didn't even need to write that age-old principle in my notebook. Clarice would be proud of me. If it worked.

CHAPTER 8

It took me close to an hour to find the main house. I thought I followed Walt's directions, but navigation has never been my strong suit. But the time wasn't wasted.

Blue gaps started appearing between the clouds, and slanting rays winked amid thick trunks in moist, sparkly shafts. The tree branches still dripped a soft patter, almost like a polite golf applause for the spectacular display the forest was putting on. Green—I'd never seen so many different shades of green, from the brilliant chartreuse of lichen clinging to craggy bark to the black-tinged emerald moss mounded over fallen logs and stumps.

The trees came in all shapes and sizes and colors, from smoothly conical and teal-tipped to scraggly with droopy branches. It was a wild, timeworn forest and strictly volunteer, not a crop mass planted in tidy rows by a lumber company.

Between the exercise and the scenery, my mind settled on the reality of my new situation, and my to-do list grew. Once I identified action steps, I started feeling better, more purposeful and less lost.

I did a quick check for sneaky farm animals in the vicinity before pulling open the kitchen door.

Clarice was bent over the sink, scrubbing, her elbows pink from the exertion. A giant handkerchief scarf printed with neon lemons and limes bound her bouffant, and she had a ruffled red apron tied around her middle. The floor shone with wet patches, and I froze, my foot dangling a few inches above a cream-colored tile.

"Don't bring those muddy boots in here," Clarice growled without turning around.

"Yep," I replied, hopping to keep my balance. I leaned on the doorframe to untie my laces.

"You need to get rid of that rental. Racking up unnecessary expenses. We'll have to implement austerity measures."

"Yes," I said slowly. I'd already come to the same conclusion. But when Clarice barks orders in that tone, something's irritating her.

"That urchin came back."

"Eli?"

My comment prompted one arched brow over her shoulder and a grunt. "Has a name, does he? Squirt about scared me to death. Brought that." Clarice jerked her head, hair, and scarf toward the table.

I tiptoed into the room in my socks and picked up the small carved wood object, no bigger than a golf ball. It was a bright-eyed, perky little brown bird—maybe a sparrow?—with a round hole in its open beak and a slotted hole in the tail. A whistle. Just the type of treasure a boy would carry around, but the delicate carving had to be beyond Eli's skill set.

"He didn't say a word," Clarice huffed. "But it was clearly not meant as a present for me. Those blue eyes don't miss a thing. He was looking for you."

I slipped the whistle's leather thong lanyard around my neck and gave a test puff on the bird's tail. It warbled—sweet and high and delightful.

Clarice wiped her hands on the apron and came over for a closer inspection. I held the bird out to her, and she stroked it with a tentative finger. "Beautiful," she murmured. "Who'd have thought? I wonder where he got it?"

I'd already ruled out Walt because he was direct and unpretentious and would have given me the whistle himself if he'd wanted to. The only other person on the premises who might be capable of such craftsmanship would be the hermit. Clarice already had enough worries. I didn't want to bother her with the tale of a reclusive man she would most likely never meet. I shrugged and let the whistle drop against my chest. I'd wear it until I could thank Eli properly.

~oOo~

A stairstepped group of shy, lanky boys in desperate need of haircuts and toting an assortment of brooms, mops, and buckets showed up just as Clarice and I were wrapping up a feast of tuna salad on saltines complimented by V-8 juice. Next time we went shopping, I was going to handle the menu planning. I honestly don't know how Clarice keeps her barrel-shaped figure on such meager fare.

The tallest boy, maybe fourteen or fifteen, took charge, announcing they had come to clean in a voice that cracked. He coughed into his fist and merged back into the group, blushing.

"Right ho." Clarice zipped my paper plate away just as I lifted my last cracker. "Follow me."

She marched through the far doorway and up a half-flight of stairs, the boys straggling after her. I took up the rear.

When we'd clustered at the end of a long, chilly room, barely lit by sunlight peeking through cracks in what appeared to be floor to ceiling drapes along one wall, Clarice leaned in like a quarterback in a huddle.

"We'll clean only what we need," she said. "Two bedrooms and a bathroom, plus the kitchen which I've nearly finished." She turned. "You and you—" she pointed at the two biggest boys, "come with me. The rest of you start near the fireplace and work this direction."

The young boys scrambled off as if they knew exactly what she was talking about. I followed Clarice and the taller boys up another flight of stairs. We turned a few corners and went down a short hall.

"These'll do," Clarice announced, pointing at two open doors opposite each other in the hall. "Pick."

Her intent look in my direction meant she was talking to me. I gestured to the right.

"Good. Let's get these cleaned up. We can sleep on real beds tonight."

The room was hardly bigger than my dorm room in college. It was crowded with two single beds, a nightstand with a lamp between them, a four-drawer dresser and a single ladder back chair.

"We could move out one of the beds," ventured the tallest boy.

His eyes, with lashes as long as a girl's, were level with mine, and I suddenly felt old—old enough to be his mother. "Good idea. What's your name?"

"Dill."

"Like pickles?" I asked.

"Like Bob Dylan. Everyone shortens it."

I laughed. "You don't mind?" I also breathed a slight sigh of relief. Dill's parents had to be a little older than I am if they were impressed enough with the aging rocker to name their son after him.

Dill shrugged and grinned. He proved to be a boy of few words, which suited me fine.

We worked in tandem, lifting the bed and crab-walking with it down the hall to a larger room that was already stacked with miscellaneous furniture.

I lost count of how many buckets of dirty water we emptied and refilled with short-lived clean water. I scooted the chair around the periphery of the room, wiping down the walls and sending clouds of dust billowing. Dill polished the window until it became translucent, then he propped it open to let in the sweet, damp air.

I sniffed appreciatively. Is it possible for the absence of scent to be a scent of its own? It had been so long since I'd been in a place where car exhaust, city sewers, and masses of people hadn't influenced the air I was breathing.

Dill noticed. "It's from the storm last night. Brought out the sap."

"Sap?"

"From the trees. That piney, sweet smell. Sawdust smells like that too, when they chop the trees up. Ever been stuck behind a sawdust hauler on the road?"

I shook my head.

Dill shrugged—one shoulder this time. Clearly, I had missed out on something amazing.

Clarice popped her head through the doorway. "Good. I'll bring clean sheets in a jiffy."

"Sheets?" I was starting to sound like a parrot.

"Found a linen closet and the biggest laundry room I've ever seen. Those washers were built to last." Clarice's lips pursed into a tight, lipsticked frown. "Kept myself occupied while you were out rambling this morning."

I held up my right hand as though I was swearing to tell the whole truth and nothing but the truth. "As instructed, remember? But no more shirking, I promise."

Clarice grunted and disappeared.

"She always like that?" Dill asked.

"Yep. But you always know where you stand with her." I grinned at him. "A trait I particularly appreciate."

He snorted softly. "You wanna see something?"

"You bet." I've learned to pay attention to these kinds of requests from children. I generally turn down the offer if it comes from an adult male. But with kids it's always a surprise and a peek into their internal workings, what they think is important. I've been shown a pet tarantula, a pet gecko, a pet stick, numerous collections of shells, pebbles, gum wrappers, dried corn kernels, et cetera, and the one that just about broke my heart—a drawing of an orphan's hoped-for family outside a grass hut. She gave me a complete narrative about their heights, ages, daily chores, and the clothes they'd wear. They were holding hands, enormous toothy smiles on their faces. The little girl had AIDS. She never got her family.

Dill retraced our steps down the hall and turned left into a darker hallway that was three times wider—a main artery in the building—to another staircase. We climbed two more stories in the gloom, a dingy window at each landing letting in enough light for me to see a thin trail of footsteps in the dust. Dill had apparently been this way before, more than once. What boy wouldn't want to explore an eerie, old, abandoned mansion?

The staircase was grand in the truest sense, like the set of Tara for *Gone with the Wind*, with a massive, polished wood balustrade. Built long before contractors cut corners with newfangled, cheaper materials. She showed her age, but her bones were good. Put in a few ornate chandeliers and clean her up, and she'd be ready for a ball.

Dill turned down an identical large hallway—they were stacked on top of each other, one on each floor—then pushed open a creaking door into a low room with an angled ceiling. He went straight to the three peaked dormer windows at the far end and rubbed a clean spot in the central window with his sleeve. "Painted shut." He stepped back.

I pressed my nose against the glass and forgot how to breathe.

The sun had broken through, highlighting miles and miles of forested hills. They stretched to the horizon in diminishing shades of blue-green. To the left, a flat-topped, snow-clad mountain rose out of the rolling evergreen breakers like a tabletop plateau. Straight ahead, another snowy peak. They were so brilliant they shimmered close, like a mirage. I wanted to stretch out and touch them, let their crystal ice drops dribble through my fingers. I shivered involuntarily, as though blasted with the glacier cold they implied.

"Like it?" Dill asked, his voice anxious.

"Wow," I breathed. "What are their names?"

"St. Helens is the short one—you know, the one that blew up. The other's Adams. You can see them from other places on the farm, but this is the best."

I turned to him. "Where were you born, Dill?"

He shrugged, eyes downcast, lashes dark against his cheeks. "Don't know."

"What do you remember?"

"My mom and I always stayed with other people, in apartments or motels or sometimes in bus stations and homeless camps if she couldn't find anyone to take us in."

"So this?" I tipped my head toward the window.

"Freedom," he whispered.

I squeezed his shoulder. "Yes it is, Dill. For me too." I blinked back tears. "Thank you."

Dill shoved his hands in his pockets and kicked the heel of one boot with the toes of the other.

"It's all right," I said. "I'm not always this sappy. Do you know how to make hospital corners?"

CHAPTER 9

With Clarice leading the boys on round two against dirt, I settled at the newly cleaned kitchen table and spread out. My laptop, Skip's laptop, a notebook, my phone, and a few ideas.

I listened to my mother's tangential voice mail message—the usual chatty gossip, this time with wedding flavor. Who wore what, said what, was offended by whom and/or by their placement at the reception, ad nauseam. No need to return the call, as Clarice had predicted.

I checked my watch. Dad's afternoon nap time. I'd visited two days before the wedding, had taken Skip along in the hope that Dad would make the connection with what I'd been telling him for the past few months, that I was getting married. Dad had been alert enough to play a decent game of chess with Skip, but when we left he called me Doreen—his sister's name—and after some fumbling came up with 'young man' for Skip.

I'd waited until Dad was settled in the care facility to accept Skip's proposal. I'd needed to know he was taken care of before I could think about committing myself to someone else. I sighed, my stomach in knots. At least Dad wasn't aware enough to understand, and be troubled by, my current predicament.

I dialed the nursing home's Alzheimer's unit desk, and Arleta, my favorite nurse, answered. "How is he today?"

"Tired and a little out of sorts. Still managed to complain about his chocolate pudding at lunch, though."

I smiled. Dad swears he can tell the difference between Jell-O brand instant pudding and "that cheap knock-off stuff y'all are skimping on." But he gets confused on the way back from the cafeteria and more often than not is found sitting in someone else's room thinking it's his. Good thing his fellow residents seem to enjoy the company.

"Honey, don't you worry," Arleta continued. "Alzheimer's patients don't have a real good handle on time. He won't realize you're gone for a while. He'll just be glad to see you next time you visit. How's Cozumel?"

"Warm." I cringed, hoping it was enough of an answer.

"Course it is, honey." Arleta laughed the deep-throated gurgle I love. "That's what those bikinis are for. You just keep on having a fabulous time."

"Give Dad a hug for me."

"You know he won't tolerate that, but I'll tell him you called."

~oOo~

Eight boys and the package of Oreos they decimated in under thirty seconds indicated the kitchen table was not the best location to commandeer as my office. I pulled my laptop to safety just in time, barely dodging a shower of sticky crumbs as the boys pried the cookie layers apart and shouted with their mouths full.

Their awe of Clarice had worn off, and they were clamoring over each other to impress her with tales of the strangest things they'd found in their various tenures on the farm—a cast iron bathtub with a sapling growing up through the drain hole, old tractor tires, horseshoes, a rusty revolver. I sat there, hugging the warm laptop to my chest and grinning. There is no better noise than that made by happy, free-range boys.

Clarice shooed them out the door and dropped into a chair across from me. "So?"

"Passwords." I shook my head. "Not the usual suspects—birth date, mother's maiden name—"

"Which one?" Clarice snorted.

At my scowl, she sniffed. "Uncalled for. Sorry. Did you try your info? He might have switched to the numbers of the most important person in his life."

"What, 36 - 24 - 36?"

I don't catch Clarice off guard often, but it's worth it when I do. She hooted then dissolved into bouncing jiggles and pushed her glasses up on her nose. "Are you?" she managed.

"Not for the past decade or so. There is something about spending most of my time on a rolling office chair that develops an affinity—my bottom with the width of the seat."

"You got that right, girl." Clarice smacked her own hip which overhung the side of her current chair. "You have the rest of Skip's luggage in the Tahoe? Let's go through it. He was so forgetful, he had to have written down the passwords somewhere."

So much for our new tidiness. We dumped the contents of Skip's suitcases on the floor in my bedroom. The man had packed enough changes of clothes to last a month. His scent—bay rum aftershave and shoe polish—flooded over me. I sank cross-legged into the middle of the pile and picked up a pair of white athletic socks balled together. I hadn't even had a chance to do his laundry yet, and he was gone.

Clarice gripped my shoulder. "Hold it together. Check the pockets."

The room looked like a fickle teenage girl's with clothes strewn everywhere by the time we'd examined every garment—and found nothing except ticket stubs from the symphony Skip and I had attended a couple weeks earlier.

Clarice started prying the cushioned insoles out of Skip's shoes. I pulled his shaving kit onto my lap and unloaded the toiletries. The usual—deodorant, shaving cream, razor, toothpaste, mouthwash, a trial-size bottle of Tylenol which I verified was really just filled with pills.

The only oddity was an elaborate nail care kit in a zippered leather case. A couple pairs of snub-nosed scissors, different sizes of clippers, tweezers, a knife-tipped wedge thingy, and several items that looked like dental tools all held in their designated spaces by little elastic bands. I've had plenty of manicures, and they were nowhere near this complicated. I doubted the set would have made it through airport security if we'd flown commercial. I held the case up for Clarice to see, and frowned as one side of the case flexed but the other didn't.

I had the tools out in an instant and ran my fingers over the seams on the stiff side. I hooked an elastic loop with my thumb and yanked. A Velcro ripping sound, and the case's lining came away. A booklet slipped out, its edges thumbed with wear.

I'd seen Skip with this little brown journal once. We'd been at a restaurant, and I'd gone to the ladies' room. When I had returned to the table, he'd been jotting notes in it. He'd palmed it and slid it into his shirt pocket when I walked up. He'd suggested we go for a stroll on the bayfront which made me happy, and I hadn't thought any more about it.

Skip was the king of notes—Post-its all over his desk and on the mirror in his bathroom, slips of paper magnet-pinned to his fridge, clipped to the visor in his car. One of his endearing quirks.

All those memory triggers did their job, because I got flowers from him on every possible commemorative date associated with our friendship first, then our romance, and as thank-yous for every new orphanage or charity I signed up for the foundation to support. He loved to celebrate, and he wrote notes to make sure that happened.

Clarice knelt beside me and breathed over my shoulder. I flipped a page, then another and another, faster and faster. Columns of Skip's scratchy writing, but disjointed letters and numbers, nothing meaningful.

The word *shark* jumped out, and I scrabbled back a few pages to find it again.

M Shark   070812   5.55m   103112   IND

Upon closer examination, there were a few recognizable words among the lists. *Shark* made several appearances, along with *Fat, Nose,* and *Ocho*. In fact, there was a *Fat A* and a *Fat H*. Apparently, shady operators aren't immune from the general obesity epidemic.

They were nicknames. And some of them matched up with the names Matt had mentioned.

Not good. So very not good.

I glanced up at Clarice. Her penciled brows were drawn together in a worried line.

"I'm in trouble," I whispered.

She just nodded. Then she pushed herself to her feet. "We have to get you set up, wired in. Tackle this professionally. You need a space."

"I know the place. Upstairs—in the attic. Can you help me haul a table?"

"There's an elevator," Clarice said. "The boys showed me."

"Do you trust it?" I frowned.

"Nope."

I hoped Dill wouldn't mind, but I wanted all signs of my nosing into Skip's—and now my—mess out of sight of the FBI should Matt keep his promise to return. We found a decent, only semi-wobbly table, an upholstered armchair that hadn't leaked too much stuffing, and a lamp with a working light bulb and arranged them within cord's reach of the only electrical outlet. I tacked blankets over the windows in lieu of curtains. I didn't want anyone outside to see me burning the midnight oil.

"You're going to freeze your tushie off," Clarice announced, hugging herself and rubbing her arms even though she'd developed a sweat sheen from all our stair climbing.

"It'll keep me from falling asleep." But I saw my breath puff in short spurts as I spoke.

"Coffee." Clarice turned toward the door. Her steps were slow, not her usual indefatigable marching cadence. And I remembered she'd hardly slept, if at all, the night before.

"Go to bed," I said. "No point in staying up with me."

She returned a few minutes later with a steaming carafe and a plate of apple slices spread with peanut butter. "I'm setting my alarm for 5:00 a.m. I'll come check on you then. And girl—" she sandwiched my face between her palms, "you get 'em. Whoever's done this to Skip—you get 'em. I can't believe he'd be involved willingly. Maybe they had some kind of power over him, extortion or blackmail. Get them where it hurts."

I nodded, my cheeks still squashed between her hands. "That's what I intend to do."

CHAPTER 10

I wasted an hour trying to piece together passwords from the jumble of letters and numbers in Skip's notebook. Then I went back to Clarice's advice and made a list of my information—birthday, address, phone number, my name in different configurations. No luck. I played with combinations of Skip's and my initials.

Dates were so important to him, so I veered into that track—the day we met, the day he asked me to head his foundation, our first date—which was supposed to have been dinner at a venerable Italian restaurant but ended up as a progressive meal of burritos and cotton candy on a pier because a political protest clogged the street where the famed cafe was—the day he proposed, our wedding date.

Then I tried the date he first told me he loved me, written out to get the right number of characters—August17.

Bingo.

I pushed back in the chair and sat blinking as Skip's private folders stacked up on the screen.

A few were clearly labeled as Turbo-Tidy Clean files—tax records, expenses, purchase orders. The rest, hundreds of files, were named with codes that were starting to look familiar. I picked one at random and clicked it open—and gulped at the astronomical sums that bounced back and forth across the debit and credit columns. I checked others, and others, and others—while the details were different, the concept was the same. A mind-boggling amount of money had been shuffled. Turbo-Tidy Clean's net income was chump change compared to these numbers. The company was being used as a front.

Skip's claim of hopelessness at balancing his checkbook—that had to have been a ruse, feigned. There was no getting around it—a patent lie.

My body dwindled into slow motion as the realization sank in—my vision blurred, I forgot to breathe, the exact way Skip had looked across the desk during my interview when he flushed a little as though he was embarrassed to tell me he wasn't good with numbers—the scene rolled sluggishly across my mental screen.

He'd said that he much preferred the marketing and operational aspects of his business, that all he really cared about was growing the foundation to help kids who were facing the same difficulties he'd had in life. I'd fallen in love with his goals right then, even though it'd taken longer to fall in love with the man himself. But I'd always assumed that was my fault since I hadn't been looking for love or a husband when I interviewed for the job. The thought hadn't even crossed my stubbornly practical mind.

Time was wasting. I jerked my attention back to the task at hand. I'd save the grieving for later. Not to mention a severe tongue-lashing for being so gullible.

These internal accounts had to be linked—the system was too complicated to allow for manual entries in all the different ledgers. I'm not a forensic accountant, but it was obvious there had to be a master entry sheet somewhere.

I found it just as Clarice padded into the room in a voluminous purple robe, bearing fresh coffee, a bowl of hard boiled eggs and a salt shaker. I greeted her with a huge grin. Except the dismal breakfast deserved some comment. "Doughnuts? Bacon? Hollandaise sauce?"

"You got in, then?" Clarice's bloodshot eyes widened behind her glasses.

"I need a few more hours. Now for the fun part. I need to do this fast—there might not be much time before someone notices. Help?" I stood and offered her the chair.

Clarice sank into it. "Tell me what to do."

I set my laptop in front of her and brought up the foundation's list of supported charities. Then I sat on the floor with my back against the wall and balanced Skip's laptop on my knees. "Open all the orphanage accounts. You know how Skip makes a monthly deposit to the foundation from the business? I'm about to make that funnel a whole lot bigger, but the funds can't stay in any one place very long. I'm going to set up streams to filter it through several charities per continent."

"Speak English," Clarice muttered.

"Read me bank account numbers. Start with southeast Asia."

Wire transfers had been foreign territory for me too when I'd started working for Skip's foundation, but now it was routine. With a few clicks and an e-mail to Anna, our bank service representative who seemed to work 24/7, the floodgates opened. I needed her expert guidance because I couldn't afford any glitches. Her contacts would speed up the process. She sent back an enthusiastic response when I told her we were making special donations early for Christmas.

I crossed an ethical line, a big one that would probably send me to jail. The foundation was no longer squeaky clean, but if I was going to abscond with my husband's dirty money I might as well pass it along to worthy organizations where I knew it would be used for good. This money had gotten him kidnapped, for reasons I didn't understand. Shaking it up just might get me some answers.

I directed the money laundering accounts into Turbo-Tidy Clean's main business account and then into the foundation and then into charities all over the world. I deposited money into the accounts of almost all our usual recipients in a series of transactions small enough to be under the radar. But I couldn't leave the mysterious funds there and implicate innocent people.

Once the money laundering accounts were empty, I went back to the charity accounts where I had access and set up reroutes from one to another several times over, making sure the funds zipped in and out of different countries so the trails would be harder to trace. As the confirmations started streaming in, I composed an e-mail notifying the affected charities of a little confusion with our accounts, telling them not to worry if they saw a few fluctuations but to enjoy their Christmas gift. I also asked them to cash out the deposits as soon as their local banks allowed. I was using banks I'd used many times in the past, so I was hopeful the funds would be available soon.

Wired funds can be seized. Suitcases full of the local currencies would be a whole lot harder to retrieve. Speed was of the essence.

I became aware of a dull thudding. It sounded like an off-balance washing machine knocking about in the bowels of the old mansion. I squinted up at Clarice. "What is that?"

She bolted upright, her ears pricked. "We have company."

I gasped. "Not now. Matt cannot see this. Doesn't the man sleep?" I flapped a hand frantically. "Stall."

Clarice charged out of the room, her robe billowing behind her. The whole floor shook as she rumbled down the stairs, and I frantically selected the email addresses of my orphanages and hit the send button. I tapped out a separate message for a few pivotal charities and sent that one off with a silent prayer.

I shut everything down, unplugged the wi-fi hot spot device, coiled the cords and piled all the equipment on the table. Then I yanked a blanket off the window and draped it over the evidence. Not exactly subtle. I could only hope Matt wasn't carrying a search warrant.

I scooped up the empty carafes and dishes—they'd be a dead giveaway that we'd recently been spending time in this dusty old attic. Plus we'd left footprints all over the floor. The best I could do was close the door and tiptoe down the stairs.

At the first floor landing, I realized I needed a reasonable explanation for my delayed appearance. I ducked into the bathroom, ripped off my clothes, and stood in the tub. I spun the handles and bit back a scream as freezing water blasted over me. I tugged the brittle shower curtain around, too late to prevent a good-sized puddle on the floor.

The bathroom had last been remodeled in the 1950s with Pepto-Bismol pink fixtures and flowered tiles. Apparently shower stalls were not yet in vogue then—or the room wasn't plumbed for one. I pulled the handheld nozzle from its overhead clamp and rested it on my shoulder. The curtain clung to my wet calves, but the water was slowly warming and starting to feel good. How long had it been since I was clean?

No one was banging on the bathroom door yet, so I lingered with the bar of soap and trial-size shampoo Clarice had left on the tub ledge. Clutching a tattered, formerly-pink towel around myself, I scooted down the hall to my bedroom and discovered that I hadn't moved my own luggage upstairs yet. I snatched Skip's robe off the floor and pulled it on, cinching the belt tight.

If Clarice was dealing with our visitor in her robe, I might as well appear in similar garb. Not that I had a lot of choice. But maybe Matt would get the hint that it was far too early for a polite social call. I rolled up the sleeves and donned a pair of Skip's socks for good measure.

I crept down the last flight of stairs and steeled myself for the lies I would have to tell Matt. Then I pushed open the swinging door into the kitchen.

The person sitting at the kitchen table with Clarice couldn't have been any more different from Matt Jarvis. First of all, it was a woman, and she was gorgeous. Black wavy hair that reached her waist, creamy tan skin, enormous brown eyes fringed with Elizabeth Taylor lashes, perfect makeup and brilliant white teeth as she laughed and chatted. She was also gigantically pregnant. So big, in fact, that I immediately imagined her tipping over frontwards if she tried to stand up.

She flashed a smile my direction.

"Sidonie Gonzales, meet Nora Ingram—Sheldon." Clarice hung my new last name out there on a hyphen as a second-thought addition. "Sidonie is a sales representative for the Petal Hydration line of skin care products." Clarice raised her mug and gave me a meaningful one-eyed glare from behind it.

That's when I noticed the wheeled case parked beside Sidonie's chair. If there was one thing I hadn't expected to encounter out here in the boonies, it was a multilevel marketing pitch.

"Also bath salts." Sidonie stretched to unzip her case, grunting softly. "Lotions, lip balms, sunscreen, body scrubs, you name it. I could give you a fifteen-minute face mask, or we could go whole-hog on the full body treatment." She beamed at me hopefully. "You're my first potential customers, and it would be so helpful if you'd let me practice on you."

I didn't dare glance back at Clarice. But anything was better than facing the FBI just now. And I was dressed for the occasion. I plopped into the spare chair and sighed. "We don't have any money." I didn't mention that I had just stolen a whole lot of someone else's money.

"Really?" Sidonie frowned for the tiniest fraction of a second, then dismissed my objection with a finger wave. "Doesn't matter. I got most of this starter kit free. A promotion the company was running to sign up new representatives. I'll start with your brows."

"What's wrong with my brows?"

Clarice snorted into her coffee.

Sidonie heaved herself to her feet. "Oh, nothing. Well, not much. Just a little—I can fix it." She moved amazingly fast for her condition. She leaned over me, her belly rubbing uncomfortably against my shoulder, wielding a pair of pointy tweezers.

I scrunched my eyes closed as she tipped my head back and thought maybe she knew what she was talking about. I wouldn't mind looking more like her.

A few relatively painless plucks later, Sidonie turned and lined up a phalanx of pastel-colored bottles on the table.

I opened my mouth.

"Etherea told me," Sidonie anticipated my question breezily. "Well, first my husband said he'd seen you in the store. So I made a point of remembering that I'd forgotten something and drove into town to get the details from Etherea myself. It's not often we get new people here. Hank and I've been here less than a year ourselves, but I'm going stir crazy. This place is downright claustrophobic compared to Fort Worth." She rolled her eyes and gave an exaggerated sigh. "But Hank got a good job offer, so here we are. I'm so excited to have girlfriends. Etherea's nice, but she's not—well, you know." She slapped some cold, creamy stuff on my face with a paintbrush. "Isn't this fun?"

So the man who'd given me a momentary fright in the store was Hank, Sidonie's husband. And the cute little girl was theirs. I breathed a sigh of relief that he hadn't passed on my suspicious reaction to his wife. "When are you due?" I asked.

Sidonie patted her belly. "Any time now. I wish they'd hurry up."

"Driving over our potholed road ought to do the trick," Clarice muttered.

I tried to kick her under the table, but my leg wasn't long enough. "Twins? Where's the nearest hospital?"

"Longview, but there's a clinic in Woodland. We're not counting on making it to either one in time. CeCe came in thirty-five minutes, so I have all the supplies. Etherea said she'd help. She's only twenty minutes away."

General store manager, midwife, what else? Seems if a woman chose to live out here, she had to be a jill-of-all-trades. "How far are you from us?"

"Just over." Sidonie gestured vaguely in the direction opposite town. "We're next door neighbors. Can't miss it. I painted the mailbox with reflective yellow paint."

Clearly, I had missed it the afternoon I arrived in the pouring rain. If I'd seen a neon mailbox, I'd have certainly stopped to check. "You'd better have my phone number, just in case. Not that I would know what to do, but I could hold your hand, heat water, or something."

Sidonie laughed—a bright, pleasant trill. "We'll manage. But I might need someone to watch CeCe."

I grinned. "Definitely." I'd pick up a few packets of Skittles on my next shopping excursion. I figured that would instantly make me a favorite with the little girl.

Sidonie was a great conversationalist. Between exfoliating, masking, and moisturizing, she filled us in on all our neighbors (three), what she knew of Walt and the boys (next to nothing, 'private' she called them), what kind of shopping and services we could find in Woodland, and how frequently it rained (all the time).

"Did you know this place was once the Mayfield Poor Farm?" Sidonie asked. "Named that since we're in May County. Can you imagine living here in the old days? I heard it was dormitory style, and the residents were locked in at night to keep them from stealing stuff and running off with it." She flushed. "Oh, I didn't mean—I'm sure it's nicer now."

"Not really," Clarice grunted. But she relented and allowed Sidonie to give her a hand massage with tantalizing apricot-scented lotion while a peel was working its magic on my pores.

And that's how Matt found us. He didn't even knock. Just walked in.

And got what he deserved for not observing social protocol—the astonishing scene of three women, two of them clearly not fit for public viewing, one of them slumped in her chair snoring softly while the spectacularly pregnant one held her hand, containers of potions strewn all over the table amid empty coffee cups, and me with seaweed-green gunk on my entire face except for pale eye holes. I'd never seen a man look so uncomfortable.

His eyes darted from side to side as though he was considering a retreat. But then he jabbed a stern finger at me. "I need to talk to you."

"I'm a little busy."

"Now." He glared and backed out of the door.

Apparently it had to be a private conversation. I sighed and shook my head at Sidonie's wide-eyed glance. "Long story," I whispered, and followed Matt outside.

"You look like an alien." Matt's brow wrinkled in consternation—or suspicion, his eyes narrow.

I decided no retort would be the best course.

"I have news. It might be good." Matt carefully studied the dirty passenger door of his government-issued muscle sedan. "Or not. We suspect your husband may still be alive."

I gasped and clutched his arm. "Where? Are you sure? Is he safe?"

He glanced at me and away just as fast, wincing. "No. Not sure. All the accounts he'd been using for money laundering were dumped last night and this morning. Looks like he's trying to cover his tracks."

My breath froze in my throat. So the FBI was attributing my financial foray to Skip—they were on the wrong trail, for the moment, and I needed to keep them running. I swallowed and asked, trying to keep my tone hopeful, "But you're sure it was Skip?"

"We don't know of anyone else who has access to the accounts. He had plenty of minions doing the courier work, but he was a control freak, with good reason, about the accounts." Matt squinted at me as though against a painful glare. "Unless something's happened recently to change that."

"Like a kidnapping?" I snorted. "I don't think you're as much inside Skip's head as you think you are. How long have you been watching the accounts?"

"I'm not at liberty to disclose—"

"At least a year, right?"

He flinched, just a little tick, and I knew I was close.

"You threatened Robbie to get insider information. What are you doing to ensure your informant's safety now, huh? Do you even know where he is?" I poked my finger into Matt's chest. "Things have completely fallen apart, and you have no idea why."

My voice pitched higher and I continued jabbing him with each point. "You *lost* my husband—your suspect. He was taken right out from under your noses *while* you were trailing him! You won't offer me protection. The money's disappeared. What's next?"

The kitchen door was flung open, and the squat purple bundle that was Clarice crowded the doorway with Sidonie peeking over her shoulder. If my temper tantrum wasn't enough to scare Matt off, then the fierce scowl on Clarice's face was.

He glanced between the three of us and backed around his car. "I'll be back," he gritted out.

"I want good news," I shouted as he slammed his door.

We stood there, shivering in the mid-morning mist until his car was out of sight.

"Mahhhvelous, dahling," Clarice said. "Bravo."

"It's not going to work for long." I turned to Sidonie and took her hands, holding them tightly. "But you're a godsend, giving me an excuse not only to look but also to act crazy and maybe buy us a little more very precious time."

She pulled a hand free and tapped my cheek. "Your peel's dry. I'm thinking it's my turn to listen to a little gossip." She hugged my arm and led me inside, her eyes sparkling. "He's some kind of law enforcement, yes? So handsome when he's angry."

My skin stretched in peaks as Sidonie picked an edge of the peel free and began yanking it off my face. I tried to talk around the pulling, giving Sidonie only the most basic facts and promising more information later if and when I learned anything. I didn't want to put her or her family in jeopardy.

"You have such a lovely scar," she murmured as she smeared moisturizer on my face, with special attention to my upper lip.

I snorted.

"No, really," Sidonie continued. "It gives you character, makes you interesting and mysterious. I'd have known, just from looking at you, that you were up to something exciting. Your secret—what little you've divulged—is safe with me." She giggled. "I've always wanted to say that. But what are you going to tell Mr. FBI when he comes back?"

"The truth. He'll already know by then. I'm hoping for a few more hours, then he can yell all he wants."

"I'm hoping handcuffs aren't included with the yelling," Clarice muttered.

CHAPTER 11

My theatrics bought us five hours. After we helped Sidonie pack her things and watched her jounce away in a battle-worn Volvo that seemed unfazed by our driveway, I sent Clarice back to bed and found some of my own clothes to wear.

Since I couldn't count on Matt to knock, I volunteered as gatekeeper and took up position at the kitchen table. I'd have been shot for neglecting my duty, though, because I was asleep the instant I sat down.

I awoke to soft thuds and the scent of fresh coffee. Matt set a mug near my elbow as I scratched at dried drool on my cheek. Kind of like a seaweed peel and definitely organic, if you wanted to think about it that way.

"You wanna tell me why you were up all night?" Matt settled across the table from me and slumped forward with his chin on his hands so our eyes were on a level.

"Rats," I muttered, my voice scratchy. I slurped coffee to clear the fuzz out of my head and give me a moment to formulate an explanation. Same equipment, same beans, but Matt's coffee beat Clarice's hands down. I drained the mug.

"I spent considerable time rummaging in cupboards and corners yesterday when I inspected the wiring. I didn't see any sign of rats." He wasn't exactly amused, but there was a lightness to his eyes that hadn't been there earlier.

Matt had actually been quite decent. I sighed and leaned back in the chair. "I didn't mean live rodents. It's an expression, because you're calling my bluff."

His brows arched, but he demonstrated mastery of the silent treatment.

"I have to be obstinate," I bumbled on. "It's my only hope. Did it work?" I crossed my fingers under the table.

"Hope?" Matt thunked his mug down, too hard, and coffee sloshed on the table. "I wouldn't call your situation hopeful. But if you mean did tens of millions of dollars walk out the front doors of banks from Mumbai to Mombasa, then yes, you were successful."

I couldn't hide my grin. The bank in Mumbai was important—vital, in fact—to my plan. I squeezed my fingers harder, hoping he'd also mention a bank in Prince George, British Columbia.

"We got some back though. You didn't get away with all of it." My face must have fallen, because Matt added, "Europe's big banks are generally more cooperative, and slower to process wire transfers. How'd you get in?"

I shrugged. "Lucky guess." I wasn't going to tell him Skip had used a password only I would know. I didn't want to think about it myself—that maybe Skip had somehow planned for me to be the one hacking into his accounts. "We? I didn't think the money was yours." I scowled at Matt.

"Semantics." He smiled as though he was enjoying our tiff. "The federal government has sticky fingers. You think it's yours?"

"Skip and I didn't have a prenup. So if it was Skip's, then its mine too. If it wasn't Skip's, then..." I was getting really good at shrugging.

"On that note, the man we apprehended in Cozumel—the one who was sucker punched and left behind on the beach? He was killed last night."

The news curled like a python around my ribcage. "While he was in jail?" I croaked.

"Organized crime basically runs the penal system in Mexico, so I guess it's not a surprise. But it means we're no closer to finding Skip." Matt rose to refill our mugs. "It also means that whoever does own the money you were so generous with this morning is going to find out very, very soon, if not already. I told you they're not people you want to mess with."

"I know," I whispered. "I'd still like to believe Skip's innocent. Emptying the accounts was my way of finding out."

"It could be a death sentence."

"They have to find me first, on my territory. You want to reconsider offering me protection?"

"Can't. Do you think you made the FBI's Christmas list with your little stunt?"

I stared at a dusty cobweb waving in the corner of the ceiling and shivered. The draft was coming through the kitchen door which had swung open a few inches. I got up and pushed it closed, wiggling the handle to make sure it latched.

"I left enough money to keep Turbo-Tidy Clean running for now. The employees have to be paid." I leaned on the table beside Matt. "Okay? They deserve at least a modest severance if Skip's not found in the next two weeks. I also left an additional ten million which is reserved for paying his ransom. It needs to be protected in the case of a bankruptcy. I expect you to pull strings with the judge to make sure that happens. Those are my terms."

"Terms for what?"

"Helping. I've done what I needed to do, now I'll do what you tell me. I'll be nice and cooperative."

Matt laughed, a deep rumble that started in his stomach.

That's when I noticed the dirty sneaker poking out from behind a teepee of mops and brooms in the corner. My heart sank. How much had he heard? I needed to get a padlock for the door.

"Eli? Come here."

First one blue eye, then the other and a tangled mess of fawn-colored hair appeared from behind the cleaning supplies. He scrambled to his feet and walked slowly to me. He pressed against my side, peering at Matt from around my hip.

I rubbed his back. My silent boy with the big, big eyes. My boy who knew too much.

Matt's lips pressed together in a tight line. He stared at me and shook his head, just a tiny side-to-side movement.

"Stay here," I squeezed Eli's shoulder and followed Matt outside for the second time that day.

"Any reason the news media would be interested in Skip's disappearance?" Matt asked in a low voice once he'd closed the door behind us.

"We had a charity ball to attend in mid-December. The San Francisco society columnists are always in attendance. I'll send my regrets. Other than that, no. Our private lives are hardly newsworthy."

"It's important to keep this as quiet as possible. It's your best chance of prolonging Skip's life if he's—well, you know, of getting a legitimate ransom request."

"You don't have to tiptoe around the idea." I bit my lip and glanced at the trees towering against the hills, teal and malachite greens and drifting pewter fog. "I know his odds are slim—or zero already."

"That means locals, too. Drug cartels, organized gambling, prostitution rings—they have long reaches, people everywhere. You have kids here. Be careful."

I closed my eyes against the beauty of what I was seeing in order to focus on the ugliness of what Matt was saying. "You're always alone. Don't you have a partner?"

Matt let out a surprised grunt. "She's on vacation—in the Bahamas—which was deemed more important than my vacation and therefore not canceled. I was going to do a little fishing, a little reading, a little lazing around, hike some, actually cook breakfast. But, nope. I'm babysitting you."

"Can you can make Hollandaise sauce? 'Cause if you can I'd hire you as chef and open this place as a bed and breakfast."

I got what I wanted—another deep belly laugh from Matt. I needed to make amends.

"In your dreams, Nora." But he was grinning as he climbed into his car.

~oOo~

I lectured Eli about eavesdropping, but not too vigorously. I didn't know what horrible things he'd already endured—what kind of neglect or trauma had resulted in his residence in a boys' camp at such a tender age. Those eyes—they took in everything but revealed so little, like a bottomless soul. I hugged him and thanked him for the bird whistle. He flushed a little, embarrassed but pleased, and I sent him on his way.

Clarice and I made our afternoon productive by finding Woodland and checking a whole load of housekeeping tasks off our to-do lists. We drove separately, and I returned the Tahoe to the Hertz satellite office where Clarice picked me up. We both hit our ATM daily maximum withdrawal numbers and then we went shopping. I put everything possible on my credit card since cash was going to become a precious commodity.

I figured Skip's money laundering clients would find me the same way the FBI did, so using my credit card was a moot point. I did, however, buy several prepaid cell phones and two new mobile hotspot devices with cash. I had to keep my cell phone on and with me, hoping for a ransom call, but I wasn't going to conduct business with it.

In spite of my newfound spirit of cooperation, I needed a safety net and the FBI wasn't it. My first call on a prepaid phone was to a friend in San Francisco who also happened to be a realtor. I told her where the spare key to my townhouse was hidden and asked her to remove all my personal items which were already boxed up and then put it on the market. I lied through my teeth about the sudden urgency of the decision and made up an obsessive wanderlust Skip and I had acquired. We were thinking about a far-ranging tour through South America before returning home. For all I knew, Skip really was in South America—it could be true.

At the library, Clarice photocopied every page of Skip's little journal. I'd have to turn the original over to Matt, but I wanted to attempt deciphering it myself. Then we drove around in Clarice's station wagon for a while, familiarizing ourselves with the area.

Mayfield—I liked that the property had a name—was starting to look like home when Clarice backed up near the kitchen door and swung open the car's liftgate. "We need to replace that bulb." She pointed to a lantern fixture mounted on the brick wall beside the patio.

A grimy blue plastic shopping bag hung from the door handle. Thinking it was another gift from Eli, I untied it and peered inside.

I dropped the bag and emitted a gurgling, strangled sound. A glimpse in what remained of the dim afternoon light had been enough to recognize a finger—a human finger—a man's finger.

Clarice was beside me in an instant, bending over the bag.

"Don't look," I rasped.

But it was too late. She snapped upright and stared at me, her face slack and gray underneath the slathered makeup.

"Oh, Nora." Her voice wobbled, and she swayed.

I flung my arms around her and held her tight as she trembled. I walked her into the gloomy kitchen and eased her onto a chair. Then I knelt beside her with my hands on her shoulders.

"I'm all right," she snapped. "Don't baby me."

I gave her an I-know-better look.

"Give me a minute." She removed her glasses and pressed her hands over her eyes. "Is it Skip's?"

I patted her knee and returned to the bag. With just my fingertips, I widened the bag's opening and forced myself to inspect the finger as much as I could without touching it.

It was not Skip's—skin too tan, nail cut straight instead of tapered with what appeared to be machine grease caked underneath. The clincher was the hair between the knuckles—black and wiry and plentiful. I guessed the owner of the finger was of Middle Eastern or Latin descent, definitely not Skip's mélange of northern European heritage. The finger had been separated from the hand, torn more than cut, because the bone wasn't shattered. The joint reminded me of a chicken drumstick. The blood had clotted, and it wasn't really that gross, although the Tillamook cheeseburger I'd eaten at the Woodland Burgerville was threatening to make a reappearance.

I walked to the edge of the patio and slumped against the brick wall, keeping to a forearm pressed across my middle. I found Matt's number which I'd programmed into my phone and hit the connect button.

"I have a finger," I said when he answered.

"You're giving me the finger?" He didn't sound amused.

"No—well, yes. I have one, an extra. It doesn't belong to anyone I know. I'd like you to come and get it."

"Nora?" His tone carried warning, as though the joke was wearing thin.

"Please?" I whispered.

I waited a heartbeat—two heartbeats.

"Twenty minutes." Matt clicked off.

I slid to sitting, my back against the wall, and watched the blue plastic bag as dusk descended fast, helped along by heavy, thick clouds. It was going to rain again. Maybe the bag was a figment of my imagination. Maybe it would just up and disappear. Maybe if I closed my eyes it would go away.

The bag crinkled in the rustling breeze, held in place by the weight within it. I supposed the FBI would be able to tell whether the finger had been removed pre- or post-death. What man had sacrificed—I presumed not willingly—his finger as a message for me?

CHAPTER 12

Matt's face was grim, jaw clenched, as he went about the correct handling of evidence. He'd shone his car headlights across the patio and was casting an impossibly tall shadow as he inspected every inch of the cracked concrete around the plastic bag. He'd already dusted the door handle and bordering wood doorframe for fingerprints.

I shivered, hugging my arms across my body, as I sat on the Subaru's back bumper.

"Go inside, Nora. I'll come in when I'm done."

"Whose is it?" I didn't budge.

"No idea."

"Do you think they were watching us and waited until we left to deliver it?"

"Could be."

"Maybe they got the wrong house by accident."

He either didn't hear me or didn't think the question was worth answering. I didn't think so either, but I wanted to hope it was all a sick mistake.

A huge raindrop landed on my thigh and instantly soaked through my jeans. Then another.

Matt muttered something and dashed to the open trunk of his car. He hurried back with a large brown paper pouch and gingerly slid the plastic bag and its contents inside. "There's nothing else here. Go on." He tipped his head toward the kitchen door.

"Is that young man staying for dinner?" Clarice asked as I shed my windbreaker and hung it over the back of a chair.

She was stirring a couple bubbling pots on the stove, the ruffly red apron in attendance. The brusqueness of her movements, her tone of voice indicated she was back to her normal self.

"He'll stay long enough to take our fingerprints for elimination purposes. What are you cooking?" I moved to peek into the pots. "I think he's a picky eater."

Clarice grunted. "He's going to find my fingerprints are already on file."

My mouth fell open and I blinked a few times. Must have been the steam. "Anything serious?" I finally managed.

"Disrupting the peace, assaulting a police officer." She shrugged. "I was a college student in the '60s. You could meet cute guys at protests. Sometimes the cute guys were in uniform."

"You assaulted a cute policeman?"

"He made me mad. Had me in handcuffs lying on the sidewalk, so I bit him in the ankle. Only place I could reach."

I blinked a few more times. "What were you protesting?"

"I don't remember now. It hardly even mattered then. Protesting was fun—beat going to class." She eyed me with a sly smile. "He asked me out later."

I was suddenly exhausted—and completely out of questions. I sank into a chair.

The phone in my pocket rang, and I fished it out. The caller ID showed Leroy Hardiman, the VP of operations for Turbo-Tidy Clean, who'd promised to call back when I'd asked for explanations earlier. About time.

"Nora?" His voice was muffled, as though he was speaking into his hand cupped around the phone. "Nora, where are you?" He was also panting. "Did you receive something today?"

All the bile in my digestive tract felt as if it was about to explode. "Was that you?" I shouted. "You disgusting, cruel—" I ran out of words horrible enough and banged my fist on the table. "Where is he—the man you mutilated?"

"Whoa, whoa, whoa. Not me, Nora. I got one too," Leroy whispered.

"Got one what?" I snarled into the phone. Leroy was already on my questionable list. I didn't want to give away more than I already had.

"A finger."

"What's it look like?"

He described a twin to the finger I'd received.

"Where are you?"

"My cabin—Big Bear."

So the courier had found us both in remote locations. Which also meant the bad guys did not yet know who was responsible for the money going missing. I hated to put Leroy at risk, but I hadn't known I was, which meant he was involved in some way. "What did you do?" I asked.

"What do you mean, what did I do?" Leroy switched to shouting. "I threw it in the trash, that's what I did. Then I washed my hands about ten times."

"You didn't tell the police?" I hunched over the phone with my elbows on my knees.

It was so silent on the other end of the line I thought he'd hung up. "Well, I just—it could have been a mistake, you know."

"It wasn't a mistake. It's a message."

Leroy whimpered. "I'm leaving. I have to get out of here." Panic rose in his voice, and there were thumping noises as if he was lugging a suitcase out of a closet, or repeatedly walking into a wall.

"Did you betray Skip?" I blurted. A shadow passed over, and I glanced up to see I had an audience—both Matt and Clarice wide-eyed and leaning on the kitchen table on either side of my chair. I pushed the speaker button.

"What? No. No, no, no. I just needed a little more, what with the kids being in college and all, and Josie wanting vacations to someplace warm. I just, you know, collected a commission. Not enough anyone would notice."

"The finger says they noticed."

"I'm sorry." Leroy had sunk to whining. "Tell them I'm sorry, Nora. I can pay them back, with interest. I just need a little time—" More thumping and ragged panting.

"Where's Skip," I asked through clenched teeth.

"I don't know. How am I supposed to know? That wasn't supposed to happen. Everything was going smoothly. No complaints, a couple meetings. Mixing business with pleasure, no worries. Something happened. I don't know. And now they're after me. I never did anything. I'm not the mastermind—" There was a horrible metallic screeching.

"Leroy?" I shouted.

"Garage door's jammed. I gotta go, Nora. I'm sorry. I'm sorry," he whispered and hung up.

Matt grabbed my phone and pushed buttons to see the caller ID. "Does that answer your question about Skip's innocence?"

"No." I scowled. "How can it? You heard him. Skip's disappearance wasn't planned."

"And Leroy is a credible source?" Matt snorted.

Clarice was madly thumbing through her Day-Timer. She pounced on an entry and jotted a note on a scrap paper which she handed to Matt. "The address for Leroy's cabin. I understand the electricity is from a generator and they have well water. It's way out."

"Check the trash cans for another finger," I added. "I wouldn't be surprised if he tries to leave the country, and I'd also be willing to speculate that he won't go to Mexico because of what happened to us there."

Matt made a few terse phone calls. Clarice handed me a stack of plates and silverware to set the table for dinner and returned to the stove.

We devoured the creamy casserole and green beans. Matt wolfed down three servings, seemingly unperturbed by the Hamburger Helper nature of the dish or by his handling of a dismembered finger earlier.

When he came up for air and sat rotating his mug of after-meal coffee in slow clockwise circles on the tabletop, he turned to me. "Why are you so set on defending Skip?"

I choked on the last of my beans. "It might have something to do with the fact that I'm married to him."

"But the evidence—"

"Is inconclusive, at best," I snapped. "You don't know him, his kindness. Look at me. Would you call this trophy-wife material? Yeah, me neither. Considering Skip's wealth and reputation, he could have married anyone, and yet he picked me."

Matt stared at me for a long minute. "What if he picked you because you're loyal? Because you know your way around international banking? Because you don't fold under pressure? Because you have spunk?"

"You're saying Skip's playing me?"

"He's conned some of the shiftiest criminals in the business. Maybe he's conning you too."

Clarice nudged my knee under the table.

I knew what she was asking and nodded. "It's okay. I want to get to the bottom of this."

She retrieved Skip's journal from her handbag and tossed it to Matt. I explained where I'd found it while he flipped pages. I couldn't read his face, but he didn't seem surprised. He slipped the journal into his shirt pocket and pushed away from the table.

"You have a gun?" he asked.

"No." My face must have registered my disgust.

"I don't like leaving you here alone, but I have to get the finger to the lab. Chain of custody—can't just drop it in a mailbox. I'll be gone at least twenty-four hours. Block the doors. Check the windows. Keep your phones with you. The local sheriff's name is Des Forbes. I talked to him yesterday—good man. His people would be the ones responding to a 911 call."

Matt rose, grabbed Clarice around the waist, and bussed her cheek. "Thanks for dinner."

"Well," she huffed, and shoved him away. "Get out of here." She latched the door behind him and rammed the table against it.

~oOo~

I don't suppose I slept the sleep of the righteous—more like the dreamless repair mechanism of the utterly exhausted. And it wasn't enough, not even close, but daylight—I won't say sunlight because the cloud layer acted as a spectrum filter—streamed through my uncovered window. It had been my first night in a real bed in longer than I had groggy brain cells to count.

Given the circumstances of the previous night, I shouldn't have been able to sleep at all, but absolute necessity trumped squeamishness and worry. Apparently no one had tried to kill us while we were unconscious because syncopated snoring emanated from Clarice's room across the hall.

I snuck down to the kitchen and opened a new package of Oreos while coffee brewed. Breakfast of champions, at least when Clarice isn't around. She must have washed the window over the sink, because a shaft of light backlit my ring lying on the sill and cast rays of sparkle across the ledge.

I picked up the ring and bobbled it in my palm. It was inordinately heavy for its size, a small but meaningful bond between Skip and me. Matt's comments from last night rattled around in my head. I thought I knew Skip. How could anyone be so good at separating his two lives that the one side (me) would have no suspicion of the other (a life of crime)? The warning gift last night was a clear indicator that the crime side knew about me. What if Skip had three lives, or four?

I smacked the ring back on the ledge. Entirely impractical to wear outside the cushy environment of my old life. Besides I might need to pawn it for cash if things became desperate.

Who was I kidding? I'd already reached desperate.

I scribbled a note for Clarice and slid the table away from the door for enough gap to wriggle through.

I set off on a ramble, sticking to the tire-track lane that wound deeper into the property and wondering if I'd collect a companion.

Sure enough. The kid seemed to have a sixth sense about any kind of interesting activity. Eli joined me within fifty yards, which made me wonder if he'd been watching the mansion, and for how long.

Maybe he'd seen something the previous afternoon, and I itched to ask him. But the soft, twinkly dew on grass blades and dripping trees demanded silence and contemplation. And for all his curiosity that bordered on prescience, I worried that Eli was also fragile.

He had not endured any grooming ministrations that morning. His hair clumped in tufts and stuck out in short wings above his ears. There was a trace of something reddish and crusty about his lips—I guessed from a tomato sauce based dish for dinner the previous night, chili or spaghetti. He crunched along the graveled ruts beside me, one sneaker trailing untied laces.

Thinking Eli would disappear again if I got too close to the bunkhouse, I chose the other branch of the road at the first fork. He needed time to reveal what was on his mind.

The trees closed in, arching over us, and an intense quiet enveloped me like a balm. It was the kind of quiet you feel in your bones—a deep hollowness that isn't empty, just permeating. This was nothing like San Francisco—no ubiquitous dull roar of traffic, no dogs barking, no doors slamming, no trolley bells, no sirens, no people shouting on cell phones, no helicopters chattering overhead. I was grateful for Eli's footsteps and steady presence, or the aloneness of the setting might have spooked me.

Finally he spoke. "Do you have kids?"

"None of my own. But I sure like other people's kids."

"What about kids who don't belong to anybody?"

"My favorite kind."

"The lady who came yesterday is going to have a kid."

I grinned. "Two, actually. Plus she already has a little girl. What did you think of her?"

Eli cast a brief glance up at me, his nose wrinkled, then shrugged. "Okay, I guess. Smells like flowers—a lot."

"She lives just over there." I pointed in the general direction. "I talked to her for a while. She's kind. If you need help, I'm sure she would be safe."

"Do you need help?" Another worried squint from those blue eyes and the uncanny ability of a child to get straight to the point.

I sighed. "Yeah."

"Because of that man?"

"Which one?"

Eli kicked at a pinecone, sending it skipping across the ruts. "The one riding the dirt bike."

I bit back a question and held my breath.

"He looked in the windows and even went in the kitchen for a minute, but you were gone. He tied a bag to the door handle."

"Did you look in the bag?"

Eli shook his head—vigorously, maybe too emphatically. I knelt and pressed his cold little hand between mine.

"Eli, I won't be angry. Tell me the truth."

"I didn't," he whispered. Tears welled in his eyes. "It's bad, isn't it?"

"Yes. But it doesn't have anything to do with you. Just me. I want you to stay close to the bunkhouse and Walt until this is resolved. The most important thing to me is your safety. Do you understand?"

A chipmunk charged halfway across the road then noticed us. It froze bolt upright, paws pulled against its chest, nose twitching. I lost Eli's attention as he stared back at the little creature.

I squeezed Eli's hand. "Do you understand?"

He nodded, but wouldn't look at me.

No point in pressing the issue. I pushed to standing, startling the chipmunk into a hightailed skitter into brushy shelter. I started walking, and Eli fell into step beside me.

I don't know where he came from—the man with the knife. I certainly didn't hear him, but the chipmunk had given us a thorough scolding from its hiding place, and I'd been chuckling at the tiny creature's outsized indignation and looking at the top of Eli's tousled head as if I could somehow read his thoughts through that thatch of hair and I glanced up and there he was.

CHAPTER 13

I don't know why I noticed that the knife was clean and shiny. But it was hard not to stare at it. My eyes flicked between the blade and the man's eyes. There was no mistaking his intent.

Eli and I merged. He flung himself against my side so hard my knee almost buckled. I wrapped an arm around his shoulder and imprinted my palm on his chest to hold him tight. I could feel his heart hammering through his thin jacket.

"It's him," Eli whispered.

Dirt bike man. Finger courier.

He looked like an upscale trail runner, the kind who spends a lot of money on his hobby—lean and muscular; Spandex leggings; waterproof black jacket cinched in at his waist; lightweight, flexible shoes very similar to the Merrells in the back of my closet at home.

Running would have been a good option except the man was close enough to grab us, and I hadn't even registered that he'd advanced. He twitched the knife inches from my face. There was a gleam, an excitement, in his dark eyes as though he would enjoy carving his initials in my cheek.

I'd been mugged, once, in San Francisco, and that guy was so nervous and fidgety, probably high, he'd been so distracted by my purse and any cash it might contain that he'd emptied it on the spot. I never felt in physical danger from him even though he'd robbed me. In the end, he was the one who'd run away.

This man was nothing like the mugger. His eyes locked on mine, and he jerked his chin to the side—a command.

I squeezed Eli's shoulder and started moving. We had a better chance in the woods—with tree trunks that could serve as shields, branches or rocks that could be picked up and used as weapons, an opportunity for Eli and me to separate and Eli to exhibit his ability to disappear. I couldn't take the risk that the man might also have a gun and easily pick us both off if we tried to flee down the road. Not to mention I was sure he could run faster than I could.

I stomped through the brush as loudly as possible, although I didn't expect anyone to be around to hear. I propelled Eli in front of me, about to give him a shove on his way to freedom when I felt pointy pressure low, near my left kidney. A rough hand gripped the back of my neck.

"Quiet. Keep the boy close," Dirt Bike Man rasped, his breath warming my ear.

We marched between trees linked together like a chain gang—my hand on Eli's shoulder, Dirt Bike Man's grip on my neck never lessening. Dirt Bike Man kept us moving fast, and in a few minutes I realized he was steering from the rear. We climbed a slight rise and stumbled into his spartan camp in a small hollow on the other side.

The dirt bike—but not dirty; it still had showroom shine—was propped against a craggy cedar, and a mummy bag lay crumpled in a smooth area cleared of pinecones and twigs. A blue plastic bag that looked like an exact match to the one that had held the finger hung from a low branch.

Dirt Bike Man kicked me in the back of the knees, and I slammed to the ground. Eli whirled around and got the knife brandished in his pale face.

"Down," the man grunted.

Eli huddled against me.

"You have to run, as soon as you can," I whispered in his ear.

Eli shook his head, his blue eyes determined.

"Yes," I hissed.

The man was digging through a pouch strapped under the dirt bike's seat, his head down. He could probably see us in his peripheral vision, but it was the best chance we'd had yet.

I pinched Eli. "Go!"

Eli winced, but he clung to me even more tenaciously. I was trying to pry his hands free when a loud snort and shuffling sounded in the brush.

I froze.

Eli grinned, revealing new front teeth growing in too big for his mouth. "Wilbur," he breathed and returned to grinning.

Wilbur. Was I supposed to know who Wilbur was? I blinked back at Eli.

Irate squealing reverberated off tree trunks as a pink and black and brown barrel-shaped bundle of fury charged into the hollow. I sat up fast and gathered my arms and legs and Eli into the smallest knot I could, anything to stay out of the creature's path.

The animal spun around, pawing the ground, snout outstretched in one direction, and stiff, squiggly tail in the other. Then it lowered its head and latched its beady glare onto Dirt Bike Man.

Dirt Bike Man dropped into a crouch, his face placid but eyes fierce. The odds looked even to me. I scooted backward with Eli.

Dirt Bike Man lightly bounced the knife in his hand as if testing its weight, and he rocked on his haunches. His whole body looked like a spring, and I realized he planned to throw the knife at the pig.

I opened my mouth to cry a warning, but a deep, drawling voice above me said, "Hold it," immediately followed by the unmistakable sound of a shotgun pump.

I tipped my head back to see the underside of tense arms and a long gun belonging to a man who stood behind me. An old man with a long, scraggly white beard and tattered clothes.

While all the humans in the group complied with the man's instructions, the pig had no such qualms. It darted forward and chomped onto Dirt Bike Man's pant leg.

Judging from his angry yelp and vigorous gyrations, I'd guess the pig got some skin and maybe muscle between its teeth along with the fabric. Spandex is no protection in a pig attack. The knife went flying and landed in a clump of ivy.

The pig, in a horrible flurry of grunts and snorts, chomped other vulnerable locations while Dirt Bike Man flailed about, screaming things I'd prefer Eli didn't hear. Half of them were in Spanish, but I've spent enough time in Central and South America to get the gist of his rather creative feelings.

I scrambled to my feet, pulling Eli with me, and ducked behind a large trunk.

Dirt Bike Man kicked free of the pig and grabbed the bike's handlebars. He jumped on the starter and got off to a wobbly start, narrowly veering around trees. For a few long seconds, he teetered on the edge of wiping out, but the knobby tires took hold and shot a rooster tail of dirt and rocks as he rocketed up over the rise and out of sight.

The pig actually looked disappointed. It sought consolation in Dirt Bike Man's sleeping bag, rooting its snout around until it found the opening and poked its head in.

The droning whine of the dirt bike's engine dwindled, and I drew a deep, shaky breath.

"You all right, ma'am?" the old man asked.

Upon closer inspection, he didn't look all that steady. His brown eyes under bushy white brows were faded with cataracts, and his hands trembled as he slid a lever and unloaded the shells into his palm. He leaned down, slowly, and propped the gun against a tree.

Rust spots pitted the gun's double barrels, and there was a deep crack in the wood stock. I wondered if the gun was more likely to explode than fire and was glad he hadn't tested its integrity by pulling the trigger.

"Dwayne Cotton." The old man extended his right hand.

"Nora Ingram-Sheldon." The hyphen was becoming habitual. His hand was warm and big and calloused, and all I wanted to do was hang onto it. I was trembling myself.

He didn't seem to mind, just pressed his thumb a little firmer into the back of my hand. "Relation of Skip's, then?"

"Wife."

"Well, any friend of Eli's is a friend of mine." Dwayne nodded toward the boy, who was scratching Wilbur's back with a stick.

"Thank you."

Dwayne smiled, showing that he hadn't been to the dentist in a very long time. Hadn't been to the barber or a clothing store in a long time either. Could have been a matter of inadequate finances. How do hermits earn a living, anyway? I wondered if he was hungry.

"Don't mind causing trouble once in a while, or interrupting trouble, as the case may be." A mischievous glint lit up Dwayne's dull eyes. "I take it you don't get along with that fellow?"

Eli darted a quick glance at me, and I knew he would absorb whatever answer I managed. Trying to work around a precocious child's understanding was a tricky business.

I nodded. "He's a messenger. His boss doesn't like a few things I did."

"Not fond of bosses myself." Dwayne reached into his beard and scratched his chin. He kept glancing at the bird whistle which hung on the strand from my neck. It had been jostled loose from my clothing during the skirmish.

A firm nose bumped my calf. Wilbur grunted up at me, his eyes half closed. I couldn't tell if he was calculating another ankle rampage or expressing his extreme satisfaction with the outcome of the first one. I stopped breathing, glued to the spot. Do good ankles taste different from bad ankles? Maybe he wouldn't bite a girl.

"It's okay." Eli handed me the stick. "He doesn't like to be touched, but you can pet him with this."

The stick worked magic. I probed Wilbur's fatty rolls with it and drew the end across his stubbled back while he snorted with pleasure. He sagged to his belly and lolled in the dirt, eyes closed. I could have sworn he licked his chops, already dreaming of his tasty morning snack.

"Coffee?" I can't believe how deep the hostess role is bred into me. My mother would be proud. "Would you like to come up to the house for some coffee and—" I frowned. "Well, we have Oreos. Maybe toasted English muffins and jam." I racked my brain for something more enticing for a hungry hermit.

Dwayne suddenly found the worn toes of his boots fascinating. "Not much for social calls," he mumbled.

I touched the sleeve of his canvas jacket. "That's all right. I just wanted to say thank you. Maybe I'll see you later when the FBI arrives to collect the evidence?" I pointed to what remained of Dirt Bike Man's sleeping bag. He might also have left some blood behind, thanks to Wilbur.

"FBI?" Panic edged Dwayne's voice.

My breath caught in my throat. Of course there would be a reason Dwayne was a hermit, and that might involve not wanting to be found by law enforcement. Whatever he'd done, he must still be worried about the statute of limitations. Why hadn't I thought of that sooner?

"Yes, FBI." I kept a firm grip on his sleeve and tried to reassure him with a steady gaze. "But I understand if you're busy."

"Busy," Dwayne muttered.

"If you have other things you need to do. I think the earliest the FBI could get here would be late afternoon, maybe even after dark."

Dwayne nodded slowly, his beard brushing against his chest. "I see." He bent and hoisted the shotgun to his shoulder. "I am indeed busy." He cracked a slight grin, turned, and strode off between the trees.

I exhaled hard, my cheeks puffing. Had I just encouraged a murderer, or a bank robber, or a counterfeiter to slip away from the law? Whatever he'd done in the past, Dwayne had just saved my life, and Eli's. He deserved whatever help I could give him.

"Well, Eli—" I turned. And found that I was talking to myself.

Myself and a sleepy potbellied pig.

"Where'd he go?"

The edges of Wilbur's nose crinkled, but he didn't have an answer.

I sighed down at the pig. "If you want Oreos, you'd better come with me. Matt isn't going to believe a word I say unless you put in an appearance."

CHAPTER 14

Wilbur heeled better than any dog I'd ever seen, trotting along faithfully on the promise of Oreos— apparently the most reliable motivator for boys, pigs, and, if truth be told, me. I pushed open the kitchen door and swiped the Oreo package off the table.

Clarice scowled at me over her coffee mug. But she was her usual coiffed self bundled in her purple robe, so she must have slept well enough.

I was just about to introduce her to Wilbur when my phone rang. I backed out of the kitchen, threw a handful of cookies on the ground for the eager pig, and answered on the fourth ring.

"Nora? This is Etherea. You know, at the general store? We got a delivery for you."

My stomach lurched at the idea of another body part. Poor Etherea. My presence was becoming a scourge to the neighborhood, if the widely-spaced houses and single four-way-stop intersection could be called that. "Um, did you look—uh, do you know what it is?"

"Biggest bouquet of red roses I've ever seen. Want me to read you the card?" She actually sounded giddy at the prospect. "I think they're from your husband."

I wondered how many people Etherea had notified before she called me. It didn't matter—everyone would find out sooner or later. I half expected Sidonie to come bouncing up the driveway to coo over the flowers. "Sure," I muttered.

"It says, 'Perfect. I knew you could do it. Keep them guessing. Love always, S.'"

My knees gave way, and I plopped onto the cold concrete patio. Wilbur shuffled over and I shoved the rest of the Oreo package at him.

The note sounded like Skip. He never was the mushy type. Matter-of-fact and to the point. But what was he referencing? How did he know? Or did he? Was this some other kind of sick message from an impostor? Or was it proof Skip was still alive?

"Nora, are you okay?" Etherea's voice was low, her enthusiasm gone.

I struggled to focus. "Can I ask why you got the flowers?"

"Happens all the time—well at least as often as we get these kinds of things around here. Delivery drivers have a heck of a time finding the addresses—they don't call the wilderness we live on the edge of the Dark Divide for nothing—so after they've driven around to the point of frustration, they stop at the store and I call the recipients."

"Do you have wi-fi at the store?"

"Yep."

"I'll be in, maybe in an hour or so. Okay with you?"

"Sure. I'll just keep hovering over these beauties, inhaling their scent, until you get here."

I pulled my knees to my chin, wrapped my arms around them and dialed. I clenched my teeth against the involuntary shivers that racked my body as I waited for Matt to answer, not that I expected him to.

At the beep, I rushed through my first few rehearsed sentences. I didn't want to sound like a whiner. "I met the man who delivered the finger this morning. Actually, he took Eli and me hostage for a few minutes, but we were able to get away in the woods. He left a few things behind that I'm sure you'd like to collect."

The kitchen door opened, and Clarice's fuzzy slippers—dyed purple to match the robe—appeared on the threshold. I glanced up to find a look of utter disgust on her face. She was staring at Wilbur who was sprawled beside me in a semi-comatose state, snoring softly, his head resting on the empty Oreo wrapper, his stubby legs protruding at odd angles from his enormous belly.

And I got the giggles. Better than crying, I suppose. The adrenaline spike was draining fast, leaving me weak and vulnerable to crazy thoughts. The first synapse my brain explored was the similarity between Clarice and Wilbur—not necessarily their physical appearances, although those were a pretty good match—but their penchant for biting men's ankles. At least Wilbur bit on the wrong side of the law.

I rocked backward, giggling even harder, and wiped the corners of my eyes. Clarice was looking mad enough that she might start stomping the slippers. Then I remembered why the cell phone was in my hand.

"Oh, uh—" I sniffed. "Description—you'll want that. He came prepared to go cross-country, both on foot and on two wheels. He's dressed in expensive trail running gear and riding a brand new dirt bike. Sorry, I don't know the make or model. All black—the clothing and the bike. Native Spanish speaker, I'd guess, given the way he swears. A couple inches taller than I am. Medium build, athletic. Black hair, dark brown eyes, a couple days' beard growth. Good with a knife. He might seek medical attention for pig bites on his legs." I snorted, then tried to make my tone serious. "I am not kidding. It's a long story." With big gaps in it to protect Dwayne. I bit my lip. "Um, see you later?" I clicked off.

"You have some explaining to do, young lady." Clarice grabbed my arm and tugged me to my feet.

"On the way to town. How fast can you get dressed?"

Clarice's normal speed, once the caffeine has kicked in, is turbo-charged whirlwind, so I hurried to collect my electronic gadgets from the attic. I was waiting in the passenger seat of the Subaru with the door propped open when Walt's rattle-trap pickup rolled up and he jumped out.

He crunched across the gravel and leaned into the opening, his hands on either door jam, blocking me in. His face under the stocking cap was calm as ever, but his eyes were furious and his breathing tight as if he was trying to regulate a pressure release valve.

I guess it takes involving one of his boys in a kidnapping attempt to earn Walt's straight-shooting, unflinching, laser-locked gaze. My head dropped, and I wedged my hands under my thighs, suddenly dead cold as though my blood had stopped flowing.

"I know," I murmured. "I know and I'm sorry. Is Eli—he's with you?"

"I made him promise to stay inside the bunkhouse for the rest of the day," Walt said, his voice so low I had to strain to hear it. "And night. I've learned I have to be very specific with him when it comes to rules." There was a trace of amusement in his voice.

I shot a quick glance at him.

Walt squatted down to my eye level and laid a hand on my knee. "I got enough of the story out of him to know the two of you could have been killed. I understand why you're here, and you have every right to be here. But the kids—" He inhaled, his hand growing tighter on my knee, his fingertips pressing hard. "I need details, Nora. You have to talk to me. For the boys' sake—and yours."

I told him everything I knew, which wasn't much and sounded woefully inadequate as my voice faltered. Recounting the odd snips and gaps, the facts without the reasons, frustrated me as much as it did Walt. I tapped the back of his hand, which was now clamped like a claw on my leg.

Walt jerked his hand away. "Sorry. I didn't mean—" His jaw tightened and he studied the lock mechanism on the Subaru's door.

"If I slow down at all, if I really stop to think about this, I'll be scared out of my mind. So I have to keep going. I have to keep experimenting until I flush out the real enemy. I don't know who it is, or why."

"What do you need?" The pupils in Walt's eyes were small and hard. Deep inside his mind, I could tell he was already running through scenarios, trying to solve my problem.

"I wish I knew."

"Protection. In case he comes back. I'll stay here with you tonight." He tipped his head toward the mansion. "Or you can stay at the bunkhouse. We could clear out a bedroom for you and Clarice."

"No. Please," I whispered. "We need separation. I don't think they have any reason to go after the boys, and let's not give them one. As much as I enjoy Eli's company, I think the farther apart we are, physically, the better. The FBI will come soon, and maybe they can offer help." It was my turn to squeeze his hand. "I don't want anything to happen to the boys. Please, Walt. You'll stay with them?"

He didn't answer, but the grim set of his mouth and narrowed eyes told me I'd made my case, for now.

"Did Eli tell you that Dwayne was there?"

Walt's right eyebrow shot up.

"What do you know about Dwayne's past? Any reason he might not want to come in contact with law enforcement?"

The tiniest smirk flitted across Walt's face, and he shifted to rub the back of his neck. "I think he might have a still."

"A what?"

"Making moonshine. I don't know where he lives, what he does. Sounds like you've exchanged more words with him than I have. I've just put a few things together from my observations and what Eli's told me."

"Isn't it easier just to buy alcohol?"

"Dwayne doesn't exactly go into town. I'd know about it if he did because—well, word like that would get around. I'm not sure he operates within our currency structure, if you know what I mean."

"No money."

"Every once in a while stuff goes missing from our storeroom. At first I thought the boys had wanted snacks, and I don't mind—I just want them to be honest. But when the snacks turned out to be several fifty-pound bags of potatoes at regular intervals, well—" Walt shrugged. "I think Eli takes care of providing Dwayne with basic food, but the potatoes are a business matter. I haven't figured out what to do about it yet, or if I even need to do anything. I think Dwayne means to give back. Sometimes I'll find a piece of equipment that's been fixed or a repair job to an outbuilding that I'm sure the boys didn't do. Makes me think he's sort of watching out for us."

"He was certainly watching out for me. But that shotgun—" I frowned. "He seemed very willing to use it, and he has ammo. Be careful. If someone surprised him in the woods, the person on either end of that gun might get hurt. He's awfully old."

Clarice banged the kitchen door closed and strode over to us. She was wearing an aqua pantsuit with floral scarf around her neck and sensible beige loafers, her giant purse slung from the crook of her elbow, as though we were about to embark on a day of shopping in the high street of a major metropolis.

Walt stood and nodded to her.

"Interrupting something?" Clarice asked with false sweetness.

"Nope. You're next. I'm just full of debriefings this morning," I answered, my eyes locked on Walt's. "Thank you," I added in a lower voice.

He gave me a short nod and turned toward his pickup.

CHAPTER 15

Just because Clarice looked like a well-stodgified member of the British aristocracy doesn't mean she drove like one. I gripped the edges of my seat and cast a sidelong glance at her. My recounting of the morning's excitement didn't seem to faze her, but then again, very little did.

If I looked out the window at the blur of trees, I'd lose my ability to breathe at regular intervals, so I focused on the denim weave pattern of my jeans. "Ideas?" I asked.

"That's your department," Clarice muttered. "I'm support."

"I need to spend some time using the store's Internet connection, preferably without the proprietor watching over my shoulder. Can you run interference?"

"Do bears crap in the woods?" Clarice growled.

I don't know why she likes me, but I'd dissolve into a puddle of atoms if she was on any other side but mine. I resisted the urge to throw my arms around her in a hug— she had plenty to concentrate on at the moment—and smiled quietly to myself instead.

Everything I did from now on was going to be a risk—had been for a while, actually—I was just starting to realize it. Might as well go for the gusto. Except for the boys. And Walt. There was no way I could ask them to leave. The camp was probably the only stable home the boys had had in their lives.

I ticked through my options—Skip's properties, at least the ones I knew about—but no others were so remote. There was a huge measure of security in being in a place where strangers were glaringly obvious to anyone who encountered them. In this tiny town, any new person would be noted with wary but insatiable curiosity, and this network of neighbors was a far greater web of protection than the rote anonymity city locations offered. I was certain now that Etherea would call me if anyone asked directions to Mayfield. Dirt Bike Man had probably gotten lucky on his own.

Wherever I went, I'd become caustic to my surroundings because of the attention I was attracting. If I could keep myself separate from the boys—and the property was certainly big enough for that—Mayfield seemed like the best roost, at least for now.

Clarice veered into the store's parking lot, slinging gravel against the dented dumpster that guarded the propane tanks. We lurched to a stop, the Subaru's bumper resting lightly against the wood railing of the long porch.

"Want to just drive on in?" I asked.

"Shut up." Clarice swung open her door and swiveled both hips to the side so she could keep her knees together as she exited the car. I wished Clarice's mother was still alive. I was fascinated by the woman who'd produced and trained such a conglomeration of contrasts. I grinned as I scooted out of the car in a less graceful fashion. Maybe I was a bundle of contrasts too and didn't know it.

Etherea had been right. The biggest bouquet of giant red roses I had ever seen dominated her checkout counter. Three—four dozen? I was tempted to stand there and count them, except their scent made me deliriously queasy. Skip always was extravagant with flowers.

Skip. I fingered the card. What was he doing? I desperately wanted to take the bouquet as a sign he was alive. But why would he send me flowers but not try to be with me or rescue me or—something? I swayed.

"Steady." Clarice's remarkably bony elbow jabbed into my side.

"Nora." Etherea bustled through a doorway behind the counter. I caught a glimpse of a cramped, cluttered office before she pulled the door shut. "Worth coming out for, aren't they?"

I managed a tight smile. "Thanks for calling. And for accepting the delivery."

"Wasn't a burden. How're you holding up?" Etherea fixed her warm brown eyes on me. "You sounded a bit shaken on the phone."

"How long since Mayfield was occupied?" Clarice blurted loudly.

Etherea jumped a little but turned her attention to Clarice. "Early '60s. After welfare took care of the families, the few remaining male residents were relocated and the place was used as a nursing home for a while. Got too expensive to maintain that old heap, I expect."

"No kidding," Clarice grunted. "You should see the ovens. They sure didn't clean them when they packed up."

"I have just the thing." Etherea hurried around the counter and started down an aisle with her finger in the air.

"You don't mind if Nora uses your office, do you?" Clarice bellowed. "She needs to check her email."

"Sure, sure." Etherea's voice wafted from deep in the merchandise. "Don't mind the mess, but don't rearrange it. I know where everything is."

Clarice winked at me and trundled after Etherea.

I left the door open a crack so I would have a few seconds' warning when Etherea returned. I sat in the creaky rolling chair, pulled my laptop from my tote and carefully balanced it on top of the shifting paper piles.

First, as Clarice had said, email. That way she wasn't lying for me. I'd set up several new email accounts in conjunction with my personal welfare management activities the other day. The notes in the new inboxes made me smile. Orphanages never have enough money, but the few I'd asked to report in were rejoicing over the infusions that gave them breathing room for a while.

I had to assume the FBI knew about my old email accounts, probably my new email accounts too, and the ISP addresses I usually accessed the Internet from. Hopping onto Etherea's Internet service wasn't much of a foil, but I had to try all the back alleys possible.

There was an email from the recipient I was most worried about, from a First Nations charity in Prince George, British Columbia. I held my breath and clicked it open. And read it with a fist pump and my heart thumping like crazy.

Then I scurried through Google Maps. I needed a rural spot, agrarian, near the I-5 freeway. The kind of place where truckers pulled over to sleep, but with enough coming and going that a transfer of goods would not arouse suspicion.

How could I possibly judge suitability from aerial photos that might be several years old? I zoomed in and finally chose a spot with at least twenty parking spaces and two buildings that looked like either fast food or convenience stores plus a gas station with a picnic area to the side. I copied the latitude and longitude coordinates into a reply email and hit send. I jotted down a few driving directions so I could find the place in person.

In case anyone in etherland was watching, I also spent a few minutes looking at other locations near the Canadian and Mexican borders and sent coordinates in emails to old college acquaintances. I hoped they would assume the messages were spam. Kind of fun, actually. I was chuckling to myself and wondering how many people I was sending on geocaching goose chases when a snatch of Clarice's voice—something about environmentally friendly laundry detergent—carried through the cracked opening.

I shut down the laptop and collected my things, leaving no obvious disturbance to Etherea's filing system. Behind the checkout counter, a partially unpacked box caught my eye. I dug through it, enjoying listening to the easy conversation between Etherea and Clarice as they traded housekeeping tips and compared cleaning products.

Bulky wool, a few alpaca blends—lovely yarn in luscious colors. I sank my hands into the box, rooting around for the softest skeins. I hadn't felt this kind of deliciousness since my last visit to my favorite yarn shop in San Francisco—seemed like eons ago.

"Yummy, aren't they?" Etherea leaned over the counter. "New arrivals. I try to keep yarn on hand for a few of my elderly lady customers who like to crochet afghans in the winter."

"The boys need Christmas gifts." Clarice's face split into a smile, her eyes sparkly behind her glasses.

I matched her grin and turned to Etherea. "How much? Actually, it doesn't matter. I'll take the whole box—if you don't mind my buying your entire supply."

Etherea blinked a few times, but took my odd request in stride. "Can always order more. You need needles or hooks?"

She led me to a carousel rack in the craft corner where I selected a few sizes of circular knitting needles. Gotta love a well-stocked country store.

As she was ringing up our purchases and adding them to our growing tab, Etherea said, "You know, you should go across the street and meet our postmaster, Gus O'Malley. Just thinking that if you were to get mail, it'd probably end up at general delivery over there—" She tipped her head. "Do you have a mailbox at Mayfield anymore? Could be why the florist's delivery driver couldn't find you. I also sell mailboxes—the sturdy kind that can survive being bashed with a baseball bat or backed into by a truck—if you need one."

Clarice and I shared a raised-eyebrow glance. Good question. I wasn't about to tell Etherea that we'd managed to receive a gruesome special delivery without the benefit of a mailbox. At this point, I'd prefer not to stick Mayfield's street number out by the road and make it easier for the next creep to find us.

After we bundled our on-credit purchases into the Subaru, we jaywalked diagonally across the intersection to the combo gas station and post office. We skirted oil stains on the pavement and entered the tiny glass-fronted office that was attached like an afterthought to the open service bay.

Clarice drummed her fingers on a dirty glass countertop which encased commemorative stamps in denominations that hadn't been sufficient first-class postage in a couple presidential administrations, scowling fiercely. She must have been distracted by something Etherea had said because normally she wouldn't touch anything in such a grimy place.

I was about to suggest leaving when grunts sounded from the oil change pit in the service bay, reminding me of Wilbur and his penchant for Oreos. Surely the postmaster didn't keep pigs? It didn't appear as though he checked vehicle fluids very often.

I eased to the edge of the pit and peered in. It took me a few seconds to realize that the greasy navy blue mound was actually a man—perhaps the largest, baldest, roundest man I'd ever seen. What he lacked in hair on top he more than made up for below his nose. Like Santa Claus but with a gray beard down to his waist, or what passed for a waist—the empty elastic casing sewn into his coveralls. The elastic must have been removed out of necessity. He was collecting empty oil bottles and other junk in a five-gallon bucket.

"Hello," I called.

He jumped several inches, then squinted up at me, his rosy cheeks balling up under his eyes. "Woowee, girl, you 'bout gave me a heart attack. You need to mail somethin'? I'll be up in a sec."

"We haven't got all day," Clarice announced. She had joined me at the edge of the pit, hands on her hips.

"Well now, no cause to get huffy." The man ambled over to a ladder bolted to the side of the pit. It looked far too flimsy to hold him.

"I can't watch this," Clarice muttered, but she didn't move.

The man placed one foot on the bottom rung, grasped the rails with two meaty hands, exhaled, tested his bouncing ability, then launched into a mighty lunge and made it safely one step up. It appeared the next step was going to require advanced gymnastics, so I turned Clarice by her shoulders and pushed her back into the little office.

We waiting, cringing at every squeak of the ladder bolts, until the man rolled over the side of the pit and pushed to his feet, his face ten shades deeper red than before. He pulled a giant, truce-flag handkerchief from his back pocket and wiped his entire head.

"What can I do for you two fine ladies?" He shuffled sideways behind the counter. "I'm Gus, by the way. Angus O'Malley, but everyone calls me Gus. Postmaster and Hog mechanic as well as general handyman, at your service."

"Hogs?" Maybe I'd been right about the pigs.

"Harleys. I can make your pipes sing." His eyes were laughing, but I couldn't see his mouth for all the beard.

I frowned. "My pipes are fine, thank you. Has there been any mail for Nora Ingram-Sheldon or Clarice Wheaton? We're at Mayfield."

"Oh, you're the new 'uns. Etherea told me." The man pulled open a cupboard door and riffled through the top few inches of a haphazard stack of circular fliers and catalogs. He turned back to face us. "Nope. Not even the stuff addressed to 'Resident'. Mayfield's been unoccupied so long it doesn't even get junk mail these days."

His eyes kept flickering over to Clarice. I'm accustomed to her foreboding presence attracting attention, but his gaze was directed higher. He seemed to be furtively examining her prodigious bouffant. Was he having hair envy?

"What about Walt and the boys' camp? Do they receive mail at Mayfield?" I asked.

"Nope. Have a PO box. You want one of those too?" Gus reached under the counter, then slapped a form on the glass, spinning it so it was right side up for me.

I didn't mind Etherea's informal account keeping, but I wanted my official name and identification information recorded as few places as possible just now. I shook my head. "Can we stick with general delivery?"

"You bet." Gus stuffed the form back where it came from. "Most people do that. If you give me your phone number, I'll call you if a package comes in. But mostly people just swing by to check their mail when they come into town for supplies."

Gus pinned the slip of paper with my phone number and first name into alphabetical order on a corkboard hanging on the wall beside an old pushbutton phone. Its cord dangled nearly to the floor, the coils twisted around each other from years of repeated stretching.

"Anythin' else?" Gus steepled his hands over his bulging belly.

I got the impression that he was usually jovial—the crinkle lines beside his eyes were etched deep. But something about Clarice seemed to be making him nervous. His gaze angled upward again.

He took a breath, his mustache indenting over where his mouth must be. He held it for a second, then said, "Seems I've seen that hair somewhere before."

As if hair can be a separate entity unto itself. I was tempted to laugh, but the look on Clarice's face warned me off.

"My mother was a wig maker," Gus continued. "Grew up with mounds of hair piled on head forms lined up in rows in the living room. Kind of rough havin' friends over. Got a motorcycle as soon as I could so I'd have a reason to be anywhere but at home. You remind me of— well, not in a bad way, of course. Just sayin'—" He was squeezing his hands together so tightly the knuckles were turning white.

Clarice was about to blow. I'd observed that expression once before, and the outcome was memorable. I grabbed the straps of her purse which were hooked in the crook of her elbow and used them like a tow rope to drag her out of the post office. "Thank you," I called over my shoulder.

After some initial resistance, she trotted along behind me at the full length of her purse leash. I wedged her into the Subaru's passenger seat and fished the car keys from her bag. She was flushed underneath the makeup—a dangerous, apoplectic shade. Her mouth opened sporadically, but no sound came out.

I had no idea what to say to placate her, so I didn't even try. I started the engine and pulled the Subaru out onto the county road, keeping a sedate pace.

A couple miles from Mayfield, her words burst out—first in staccato, then in a rush. "I. Am. Not. Old. Enough to be that fatso's mother."

"He meant no harm. He just has unpleasant childhood associations. I'm certain he didn't think..." I shrugged. "Well, I don't think..." I sighed and tried again. "You and Gus look about the same age to me."

Ooops. Clarice's withering glance indicated I had missed the mark. I gave up talking and concentrated on getting the Subaru through the gullies and over the ridges of our driveway in one piece.

I carried in the flowers first and plunked the heavy vase on the kitchen table. I debated telling Matt about the roses but decided he'd find out about them soon enough, especially if he returned to collect Dirt Bike Man's belongings. Clarice disappeared into her room, strangely silent and still seething, so I emptied the car and put things away.

I settled at the table with my box of fiber goodness and cast on a forest green color for hat number one. The yarn slipped through my fingers, warm and soft and soothing. Just a few minutes. I needed the mental space to prioritize my to-do list.

CHAPTER 16

My phone ringing jerked me back to the present. It'd grown so dim I could hardly see the knitting needles. If the stitch is uncomplicated, I can knit without looking, so I hadn't noticed. Where'd the time go?

I grabbed my phone. My stomach lurched—I didn't recognize the caller ID. Maybe it was Skip's ransom request, at last. "Hello?" My voice wavered.

"I'm thinkin' I need to apologize."

I exhaled. "Gus. I'm sorry about our rudeness. We're under a lot of stress just now. Clarice will be fine."

"You sure? She didn't look fine."

"I'm sure. Don't worry."

"Well I'd like to make it up to her by takin' her for a ride on my bike. Think she'd enjoy that?"

I tried not to sputter. "Next time we're in town, you can ask her yourself."

"Will do." Gus's tone returned to the cheerfulness I'd first heard that morning. "Well, look at that—" his voice faded.

"Gus?"

"Yeah, punkin." He sounded distracted or else I would have objected strongly to the casual endearment. "Some folks just drove up to the store across the way. Two big sedans and a gray, windowless van. If I didn't know better, I'd say they were feds. I'd better go. You take care, now." Gus hung up.

The early warning system worked perfectly. My phone rang again three minutes later—Etherea to tell me that a blonde woman in a suit had stopped to ask directions to Mayfield. They'd left the store in a caravan, a series of dark vehicles. Was I expecting visitors? Looked like someone had died, she said.

I forced a chuckle and assured her all was well. I mumbled something about surveying and data gathering, guessing that rumors of a housing development or other such nonsense might make the rounds in town from my intentional ambiguity. But better than hinting at the truth.

Clarice was still hibernating, and I was starting to get worried about her. She'd never been antisocial before—grouchy, yes; pouting, no. But if I could spare her the distress of another FBI evidence collection effort, I would. I flipped on all the lights I could find, layered on a couple more thin sweaters and laced up my hiking boots, then sat down to knit until the cavalry arrived.

It felt like ages before I caught a glimpse of three sets of headlights through the kitchen window. They jigged and jagged over the ruts, making slow progress. I wondered how many times they had driven past the ivy-covered gate in the dark before finding it. Maybe they had better GPS than I'd had, although it was smart of them to ask for directions. Leave it to a woman.

I stepped out onto the patio at the sound of slamming car doors.

"Nora Sheldon?" I heard her first, then she entered the pool of light from the new bulb in the porch light. "Special Agent Violet Burns." She stuck out her right hand, and I shook it. "You've met my partner, Matt Jarvis, already."

She was a tiny little thing, the top of her head barely reaching my chin. But she was prim, orderly, and all business in a perfectly-tailored dark suit and sturdy, patent leather ankle boots. Even her sleek blonde hair was pulled back in a tight knot. She would probably make traipsing through the woods look fashionable and easy.

More shadowy figures appeared behind her with more doors slamming, and I realized her crew was unloading equipment.

"Not here," I said. "I'll take you to the spot. It's a ten or fifteen minute hike from the nearest road."

Violet waved a petite hand, and the process behind her started reversing, accompanied by a few male mutterings. "Good. We need to talk. Inside?"

She circled the kitchen, keenly noting our attempts at domesticity, then turned to me, her green eyes bright and inquisitive. "Leroy Hardiman."

"Ahhh." I stuffed my hands in my pockets. "You found him?"

"At Brown Field Municipal Airport outside San Diego, as you suggested. He was trying to bribe a flight crew to fly him to the Caymans even though they hadn't met the FAA's requirement for downtime since their last flight."

That sounded like Leroy. My opinion of him had slipped considerably in the past few days.

"He turned into quite the blabber," Violet continued, "once he was apprehended and taken to interrogation. Full of information, much of which wasn't helpful and some of it absolute speculation." Her lips curled in disgust. "We're ninety percent certain he does not know where your husband is."

"I didn't expect him to."

"But he claims that Skip was tipped off, about what he couldn't say."

"Tipped off?"

Violet inhaled deeply and closed her eyes, just for a fraction of a second, then she plunged ahead. "He named an FBI agent in the San Francisco office, said the man had been friendly with Skip and was feeding him information on the side. The agent was working organized crime cases mostly, perhaps Skip's clients. I'm embarrassed to tell you this, but sometimes an agent can be turned. We're checking his assets, seeing if he received payoffs. Obviously, he's been relieved of duty."

"A mole." My heart hammered in my chest and in my ears, but I tried to keep my surprise from showing. Since finding Skip's journal, I'd known his scheme was big and organized, but the fact that he was working with someone inside law enforcement added an intriguing wrinkle.

"I'm also sorry to say I know him personally." Violet's nostrils flared slightly. "I went through the Academy with him. He was so gung-ho then, very zealous. I'd lost touch with him, but something must have happened to make him go over to the other side."

The other side. With Skip. I used to see the world in black and white, just like Violet. She had to—it was her job. But I wasn't so sure anymore. Better to change the subject until I could do some thinking on the matter. "So you're Matt's partner. I thought you were on vacation?"

She smiled slightly. "It was getting a little boring. My husband and I are both workaholics, so we didn't mind returning two days early. He has a big trial coming up."

"A lawyer? I need a lawyer—a good one, anyway," I muttered.

Violet's eyes narrowed to slits. "He's off limits. Conflict of interest, obviously." The last word was said with such severe terseness, I knew I'd hit a nerve. Maybe there'd been more than just work responsibilities that had made them happy to cut short a glamorous vacation.

I bit back a grin and gestured to the door. "Shall we?"

~oOo~

The FBI is nothing if not prepared. They packed tons of equipment into duffel bags and followed me through the woods. One of the technicians lent me a massive flashlight, but in the end I moved more by feel than sight. Tree trunks mostly look the same to me, but I remembered the ground swells and a few big roots I stumbled over while pushing Eli ahead of me.

The moon cast eerie, slanting, blue-tinged light between the trees, and my breath came in short, steamy bursts. My ears prickled with cold, and my nose was threatening to drip. Violet trudged on my heels.

"You sure you want to do this in the dark?" I asked over my shoulder.

"The sooner the better. We'll stick around until daylight to make sure we didn't miss anything. Frankly, I'm a little surprised you're not freaking out."

I shrugged. "Could've been worse. I'm just grateful to have escaped."

Violet made a noise somewhere between disgust and curiosity. "The pig—it'd be helpful to get photos, bite measurements."

"Good luck with that." I giggled. Oreos probably aren't part of a standard FBI supply kit. "Wilbur's rather antisocial." I stopped in a small clearing and panned the flashlight until it hit the torn blue sleeping bag. "We're here."

Violet barked orders, and her crew fanned out, each one with a specific job to do. I backed into the shadows with camera flashbulbs popping all around me, hoping Dwayne had made a clean getaway. I'd made my statement without mentioning his part in the drama. I think having a potbellied pig as a protagonist distracted

Violet from asking probing questions. She'd barely even registered Eli's part in the story, so I was hopeful he'd be spared an interrogation as well.

As I watched a technician preparing casting medium next to a tread mark from the dirt bike, I realized this operation was going to take hours—miserable hours stomping my feet to try to keep my toes from going numb and blowing on my hands. What better time to visit Walt than under cover of both darkness and a whole horde of FBI agents? I'd be willing to bet all bad guys were keeping clear tonight.

I snuck away unnoticed. Violet really didn't need my presence at the campsite, anyway, and I wasn't terribly eager to see what they found, especially in that blue plastic bag hanging from the tree branch.

The rutted gravel road was lonely in a comforting way—silent but not unfamiliar. I kept to the track's edge, close to the trees, my feet crunching on the already frozen surface.

It felt good to lengthen into my rambling stride, my arms swinging. I grew sweaty under my layers of clothing, and my eyes watered in the cold air. But I drew in great gulps of that same cold air, clearing out the dregs of worry and tension.

Clarice and I were still alive. Walt and the boys were still alive. There was a very good chance Skip was still alive—if the roses were an indicator, and the FBI seemed to be taking my problems seriously. I had a network of new friends on the lookout for me. All in all, it'd been a pretty good few days at Mayfield.

Except for the finger. I could have done without the finger.

I found Walt in an outbuilding—if it could be called that—near the bunkhouse. All the buildings on the property I'd seen other than my decrepit mansion were outbuildings, afterthoughts in even worse repair. It was a sloped-roof barn of sorts, or had been, and the large sliding door was open, revealing the glow of several lights and blue-dashed flickering inside.

Walt wore a full facemask and bent over a workbench, welding something. I recognized him from the worn boots and sketchy patch on the right knee of his jeans. I wondered if he'd let me mend his clothes. The boys might need some sewing attention too. They were a ragtag bunch, clothing obviously handed down only when it was straining at the seams and limbs extended several inches out of cuffs and hems. If things went according to my plan, I'd buy them winter coats, boots that fit, and a couple new pairs of jeans each.

I leaned against the doorframe and waited. Not a great idea to surprise a man who's holding a welding torch.

He leaned back and shut off the flame. He flipped up the visor, and I moved into his range of vision.

"Nora." Walt jumped up and tore off the mask. "You okay?"

I nodded. "Have a few minutes?"

"Of course. I checked on Eli half an hour ago. He was in his room, reading. He hasn't gone and done something he shouldn't, has he?"

I grinned. "Not that I'm aware of. You were like him as a child?"

Walt sighed and ran a hand through his shaggy hair. "Hard to imagine, huh?"

"Not at all." I clenched my fists behind my back, nearly overwhelmed with the desire to brush back the clump of hair that stuck out over his ear.

Walt cleared his throat and gave me a pointed look.

Right. I'd asked for this conference. "The FBI's here. Close to a dozen agents scouring the campsite where Eli and I..." I gestured vaguely. "I think they'll pack up and leave shortly after daybreak." I took a deep breath. "I have a favor to ask, but the timing's important."

Walt gave a curt nod, his lips pressed in a thin line—meager encouragement.

"Can I borrow your pickup tomorrow? I'd like to hit the road as soon as the FBI leaves."

An embarrassed, sheepish look crossed his face. His hair looked like burnished copper in this light.

It was too much to ask. "I'm sorry. You don't have to—" I blurted.

"It's fine." Walt stepped closer, those blue eyes intense. "It's just that the clutch is about shot. You know how to drive a manual transmission? It's four on the floor."

I sort of knew what he was talking about. I had memories—ones I'd tried to erase—of an urgent need to get to a friend's house for Thanksgiving dinner during my sophomore year of college and all of us piled in another friend's car that kept rolling backward on San Francisco's steep hills while we squealed and I tried grinding the thing into gear. We were stupid, and it wasn't nearly as funny as we thought it was at the time. My face squinched up involuntarily.

Walt chuckled. "You need lessons?"

"I should keep it in first all the way to the county road, right? And from there on, it will be easier?"

"Theoretically. Want me to take you wherever you need to go?"

"You can't." I shook my head hard. "Separation, remember?"

"And yet here you are." Walt took another step closer.

I scowled and backed up to maintain an arm's distance. "Because I need the cargo space. The Subaru's not big enough." I turned away. "Forget it. I'll rent a truck in Woodland."

"Hey." Walt's hand closed over my elbow. "What kind of cargo? Will you need to strap it down?"

I bit my lip. "Probably."

"I take it you don't want the FBI to know you're going on a road trip." A tiny crease appeared between Walt's brows. I was giving the man wrinkles. "I'll have the truck parked behind the mansion by 6:00 a.m. with the load straps you'll need behind the seat." He squeezed my arm, then released his grip. "Don't take it the wrong way, Nora. I just wish I could ground you to your room the way I can Eli. Seems that would be better for your long-term health." His eyes narrowed.

"I'll be careful." My tone came out more flippant than I meant it to be. I pivoted and strode out of the barn.

CHAPTER 17

I stepped into the kitchen, sweaty and nose dripping from my speed walk back from the barn, Walt's words still bouncing around in my mind—and did a double-take.

The stranger sitting at the table was obviously a woman, or else I would have taken off at a sprint straight for the safety of the FBI confab in the woods. Random people just appearing and making themselves at home in my world was starting to get on my nerves.

"You don't have to stare like that," she grunted.

I squinted, still clutching the door handle. "Clarice?" The body shape and size were right, but the head, including the face, was entirely wrong. The voice was unmistakable, though.

"Come in and close the door," she muttered, slinging back another glug from her coffee mug. "I'm not gonna bite."

"Not even my ankles?" I knew before I said it that I shouldn't, but at the moment there was no speed bump between my brain and my mouth. I retracted my neck into my shoulders, doing my best impersonation of a tortoise, ninety-percent expecting her to fling the mug at me.

Instead she burst into a deep, throaty laugh that tapered into wheezing and her hacking cough. "Sit." She pointed to the chair opposite. "Does that mean I look rabid?"

"No. You actually have a lot of Judi Dench panache with that—that—" I waved my hand toward her head. One couldn't really call it a haircut. More like a clipper job.

Clarice's hair, what was left of it, was perfectly silver, even sparkly, and stuck up all around, no more than an inch off her scalp.

"What happened?" I was envisioning some sort of catastrophic accident with an ancient washing machine or mangle or bellowing vacuum cleaner—or something. What could possibly consume or irreparably damage Clarice's hair that she had to shear off the glorious bouffant? And change the color? My brain was a little slow out of the gate as I continued staring at her.

But that was just the thing—her face was different too. Wrinkles everywhere. I'd known they were there, of course—pancake makeup not being as effective as the wearers usually think it is. But it was all gone. I saw real skin. Saggy in places but completely natural and, well—real.

I grinned.

"Decided to quit pretending. Face the music."

"Is this because of Gus's comment? He's sorry, by the way."

Clarice's brows—the real ones—arched quite expressively. "And you know this how?"

"Small town."

"Good grief," she muttered. "Should have done this earlier, before any of them ever met me."

"So you cut your hair to make a statement?"

"Girl." Clarice sounded exasperated. "Don't you know anything? It's a wig. I've worn that darn wig, or versions of it, for nearly fifty years. It was the trendy thing back in high school, and I just kept at it. My mother had expectations."

"Yours too?" My shoulders slumped.

A wicked grin crinkled Clarice's face, lighting up the wrinkles. "Why do you think I don't let you talk to yours?"

I was developing a bad habit—staring.

Clarice shrugged. "Figured since we're on the lam, sort of, I might as well ditch the masquerade. We have enough to worry about as it is. No sense in insisting on pretenses."

I nodded slowly. "I like it. Classy."

"A healthy dose of reality never hurt anybody."

Even if it was newly acquired. My cheeks were hurting, I was grinning so wide. "I think we'll need to go into town again soon, show you off. How do you feel about motorcycles?"

Clarice muttered something I won't repeat.

"Well, not tomorrow. At least not for me. I need to make an excursion. I'm borrowing Walt's truck."

Clarice sat up straighter and thunked her mug on the table. "Not without me, little Miss-Secret-Pants. Whatever you're doing, you'll need a navigator."

"Look who's talking," I muttered. "It's a secret because I want everyone to be able to honestly tell the FBI they don't know, in case they're questioned."

Clarice snorted.

And that was my answer. "Then we're leaving at 6:00 in the morning. Or after the FBI team departs, whichever is later."

Clarice rose and placed her mug in the sink. "Guess I'd better be getting my beauty sleep then." She cast a gleaming-eyed scowl at me and shuffled out of the room.

~oOo~

Clarice had the right idea. I needed to be mentally sharp and alert the next day.

My tiny bedroom reeked, in the best sense, of roses. I'd stashed them on the bedside table in my scramble to clean up before Violet and her team arrived. I dreaded trying to explain them to the FBI. I would—in time—but I had some thinking to do first.

I stripped to my underwear and burrowed under the covers, pulling my laptop in with me. The florist's address printed on the card was in Longview, the closest town big enough to also have a hospital per Sidonie. The roses had probably been ordered over the phone, or maybe online. I wondered if I could sweet-talk a clerk into sharing that information.

The FBI mole was bugging me too, and I realized I hadn't gotten his name from Violet. I pulled up the main San Francisco news outlets, but reports about a traitorous agent were notably absent.

Who did I know who knew everyone? Clarice was patently incapable of sweet-talking. My mother, on the other hand...

I rooted around for other options—friends I knew from college; foundation supporters; social climbers; Skip's business associates, at least the ones I thought were probably legitimate—and kept coming back to my mother. If you absolutely must know the latest, juiciest gossip, the place to go in San Francisco is my mother. The problem is, her shutoff valve is leaky, and my situation, if she knew it, might also become part of the rumor stream.

On the other hand, at least one of Skip's enemies already knew where I was and had found Leroy too. No doubt the rumor mill worked just as well on the other side of the law. I heaved a deep sigh. If I wanted information, I'd have to take the risk.

It was late, but my mother is a night owl. I rummaged in my tote and pulled out one of the new prepaid cell phones. My mother also always answers the phone, even if she doesn't recognize the caller ID. She hasn't met a telemarketer or pollster yet with whom she can't have a decent conversation. And by conversation I mean thirty minutes of trading life histories. I dialed.

"Hi, Mom," I said when she answered.

"Nora. Why didn't you tell me you were selling the townhouse? I know of at least four couples who would love, love, love to buy it. I could have saved you the realtor's commission, darling. Of course, there's a bidding war, so maybe you'll recoup your expenses."

"Great," I muttered. I wondered where my realtor friend had stashed my stuff. I really was going to be homeless, in fact as well as feeling, in a matter of days. My mother was still talking, but I interrupted her. "I need a favor."

The silence on the other end of the line was like someone had left the door to a walk-in freezer open—cavernous and hollow and yawning. I could even hear my mother panting, trying to catch her breath. I guess maybe I'd never asked my mother for a favor before.

"Are you all right, honey?"

"No."

At her sharp inhale, I scrambled—that's not exactly what you tell your mother, especially not a mother like mine.

"I mean yes. I'm alive and healthy—" I blurted. Slippery slope. I needed to distract her. "There's been a bit of a mix-up. I need to contact one of Skip's friends, but I don't have his information."

I explained, in the sketchiest terms because that's all I had, about a friend who'd been helping Skip and consequently had lost his job with the FBI. Clearly, the FBI wasn't going to trumpet the fact, so there wasn't any information in the public realm. I envisioned my mother licking her chops at the prospect.

I also sicced her on the florist's shop in Longview. They didn't stand a chance.

"Mom," I finished, "please be careful. There's a lot going on that I don't understand. I have to hope Skip's okay, but I haven't seen him for a few days."

"Isn't this exciting?" Mom gushed.

I blinked. It was not the response I'd been hoping for.

"So you're saying Skip is some kind of outlaw?" She sounded thrilled.

"It's not a romantic notion like in the movies, Mom." I scowled at my rumpled pillowcase. I could tell her about the finger and bring her back down to earth, but I quickly vetoed the idea. "Just be careful, okay?"

"Sure, sure, honey." But her voice had that distant quality. She was plotting her approach already.

"Give Dad a hug for me." I clicked off and flopped onto my back.

A jagged crack ran from the hanging light in the center of the plaster ceiling to the corner over my head. Just like the fault lines San Francisco was built on. Just like my life, suddenly crumbling to pieces with my marriage as the turning point.

~oOo~

Clarice and I were in the kitchen, forcing down our third mug of coffee in the past hour and tapping our watches to make sure they were still ticking when the FBI caravan pulled up outside. Violet stuck her head through the kitchen doorway, her eyes bleary and the chic hairdo drooping, flipped her card on the table, and muttered a cursory good-bye.

"Results?" I called.

"Lab first. We'll let you know." She was already climbing back into the passenger seat of a behemoth sedan that was a twin to Matt's. They made a noisy exit, engines rumbling and gears grinding over our driveway.

Clarice packs like Mary Poppins. Indefatigably prepared. She was dressed in a snazzy pair of jeans, low leather boots, and a zip-up yellow windbreaker with a stocking cap pulled over her short hair and ears. She looked like a hip grandmother, spry and ornery, but there was no way I would make that comment out loud. I was just glad Violet hadn't met Clarice the day before, or there would've been time-consuming explanations to make about the absence of the ubiquitous beehive.

When the exhaust from the last vehicle dissipated, I stepped away from my post at the kitchen window. "Clear."

We trotted around the mansion.

And there was Walt's pickup as promised, in all its rusted-out glory.

"I hope you weren't planning on a high-speed getaway," Clarice said.

"We just need to blend in, not arouse suspicion," I puffed. The driver's door was stuck. I jiggled the handle, gave it a few thumps with my fist to break the thin layer of ice, and tried again. Worked like a charm. I was starting to like this truck.

"A couple of cute girls in a redneck clunker ought to blend in fine." Clarice rolled her eyes at me.

"I haven't told you yet where we're going," I replied with a grin. "I'm pretty sure no one will give us a second glance."

Clarice hoisted herself onto the bench seat from the passenger side, picked an ice scraper off the floorboard and thrust it my direction. "Hurry up. I haven't got all day."

Walt had also left a pair of gloves—far too big for me, but I wore them anyway. They certainly made scraping the windshield more tolerable. There were a few things I hadn't packed for a Cozumel honeymoon that would have come in handy in my new situation—like a parka and mittens.

I jumped back into the cab, flicked the windshield wipers, checked the turn signals, and made sure I could reach the pedals.

"So?" Clarice grunted.

"Here goes." I took a deep breath and latched my seatbelt. "It's been a while."

If it was at all possible, then I did it—made the pickup's clutch even sloppier. But we lurched the potholed distance to the main road and picked up speed on the smooth pavement.

"Good thing I didn't eat breakfast," Clarice groaned, one hand pressed against her stomach.

"That's exactly how I feel every time *you* drive," I gritted through clenched teeth as I wrangled the gear stick into fourth.

When the truck settled into the irregular, vibrating chugging that was its normal purr, I pointed to my tote bag. "Directions are in there, but I won't need navigational help until the last few miles. Once we get through Woodland, it's a four-hour straight shot north on I-5."

Clarice seemed to forget her gastrointestinal trouble and peered at the page. "Bellingham? What are we doing there?"

"It's a secret, remember? I'm saving you from an unpleasant interrogation."

"I'm going to figure it out eventually, you know."

I flashed her a frown. "Let's put that effort into something else. I want to know exactly who we're up against. Those names Matt mentioned are a start, but I'm sure there are more. Feel like picking through Skip's journal to make a comprehensive list? If we have time, maybe we can find wi-fi somewhere and do some research. Figure out which one of his cronies is most apt to send a finger."

Clarice pulled out a notepad and pencil and began tallying, calling out new names as she came across them. An hour later, we had a list of twenty-seven potentially disgruntled former clients of Skip's. Clarice ranked them by the number of transactions noted in the journal.

"The names at the bottom of the list—can you tell if their accounts were cleared, if their funds were returned?" I asked. "I expect they would get their, well, deposits—for lack of a better term—back, but in smaller chunks over time. Do you see a pattern?"

Clarice swiped the hat off her head as if her brain was in immediate need of oxygen and bent over the photocopied pages of the journal. I wondered how she used to think at all, suffocating under the bouffant wig. She ticked pencil marks next to entries and flipped quickly through the pages.

Her soft grunts increased in frequency and excitement. I kept glancing over at her while trying to keep the truck at a steady 70 mph rumble in the slow lane. We sure didn't need the attention of a patrol cop just now, but Clarice was making noises like she might explode.

"Ha! Simple!" She tossed the pages onto the seat between us with a fierce smile on her face.

"Care to elaborate?" I swerved back between the lane lines and renewed my grip on the steering wheel. Was it my imagination or was the pickup developing a tendency to veer right?

"He used Roman numerals, nothing less than X or ten, and I'm guessing that's ten thousand."

"Peanuts," I muttered.

"I was looking only at the small accounts, remember? But the answers to your questions are yes, yes and yes. I need a spreadsheet to make sense of it all, but yes, some of the accounts look as though they're closed. He has this little symbol—see this?" Clarice waved a page under my nose with her finger angled toward a black dot. "Looks like this marks the final payment to a client."

I bit my lip. "Could you count the black dots, please? I want to know just how many accounts weren't resolved before I had my little fling."

"How many enemies we made, you mean."

"That too," I whispered.

Clarice took her time, checking and double-checking. I tried to enjoy the scenery—greens and more greens even though the deciduous trees' limbs were bare. They weren't kidding when they named Washington the Evergreen State. White frost lingered on the grass in the shadows cast by the trees.

Semitrucks barreled past us. I was having trouble keeping the pickup at the speed limit. The tired old girl just didn't have the ooomph—maybe she was good only for short sprints. So we hunkered in the slow lane and watched interstate commerce zip by. The log trucks gave me chills, their grilles like gaping maws in the rearview mirror. When they pulled around us, they buffeted us with that same sweet, sappy odor that Dill had brought to my attention, although probably not as strongly as the sawdust haulers he favored.

"Eighteen," Clarice announced. "That leaves nine active accounts."

A much more manageable number.

"But they're the biggies," Clarice continued, extinguishing my momentary flicker of encouragement. "I can't do all this in my head. When—if—we stop, I'll crack open a spreadsheet and total the damage."

The next couple hours passed slowly, too slowly, mainly due to the fact that I was wrestling more and more with the steering wheel. The alignment problem had not been my imagination. Not a surprise considering the kind of terrain the old girl regularly traversed.

"Overheating?" Clarice asked as I pulled into the parking lot of a Denny's restaurant just off the first Bellingham exit.

"Don't even think that. She has enough problems as it is."

"She?"

"Bertha. Or Maude. I'm trying to decide."

"Not Gisele?"

"That sounds too much like something agile and nimble. No, I was going more for inert and stubborn."

"I take it we're early?"

"My behind's numb, and I need breakfast."

"'Bout time." Clarice popped open her door and rolled off the seat.

CHAPTER 18

We weren't the only ones who wanted served-all-day breakfast when it was actually nearing noon. We had to wait ten minutes for a booth still greasy with the fingerprints of the previous patrons. The place was packed with retirees sipping bottomless coffee and truckers inhaling mounds of pancakes—the kind of people who either don't need to or can't afford to observe proper mealtimes. And now I was in that category too, for both reasons.

Like a couple of workaholics, Clarice and I set up our laptops back to back—me on my own and Clarice on Skip's—and ducked behind the screens. We clicked away in silence except for placing our orders when the waitress, a wan twenty-year-old in orthopedic shoes who smelled faintly of cigarettes, finally made an appearance. I was going to need the fortification of an entire side of bacon.

Clarice rose, fetched a carafe from the serving staff's supply station and refilled our mugs. On the way back, she topped off mugs at several other tables. She returned with her hands full of single-serving-sized sealed plastic cups of cream and dumped them on the table. "Eat hearty."

"Do I have to tip you?"

"A little gratuity wouldn't hurt." She plopped onto the end of the seat and propelled herself into the middle of the slick vinyl. "Just needed a dose of reality and caffeine before I showed you this." She spun her laptop around. "Bad guys one through nine, in order of the current value of their business dealings with Skip."

I leaned closer, my hands clamped on the edge of the table. Eye-popping numbers. My heart raced—the identical reaction I'd had to seeing the totals in Skip's secret bank accounts. These amounts were in the same ballpark.

I forced myself to inhale before I passed out. "Let's get beyond the nicknames. I'll take it from the top. If you'll start at the bottom?"

"The Nose. Charming," Clarice muttered. Her silver hair actually glinted under the replica Tiffany stained glass pendant lamp that hung over our table, kind of like those multicolored fiber optic novelty sculpture things that show up at white elephant gift exchanges.

"You look good, you know," I said.

My comment barely warranted a glance over the laptop screen. "Huh," Clarice grunted, but her eyes sparkled a little.

"Don't work too hard, now," the waitress said as she plunked down our plates.

"Wouldn't dream of it," Clarice said as she doused her waffle with warm maple syrup. "Nigh unto impossible."

The waitress stared at Clarice as if she was speaking a foreign language.

"This looks great," I said. "Thank you."

The waitress started as if she'd been in a trance, took the hint and whisked down the aisle.

I stuffed half an over-easy egg into my mouth and returned to the keyboard. We had to work hard—and fast. As if our lives depended on it, because they probably did. We were researching criminals in need of money laundering services. Not your typical lunch at the office away from the office.

By the time my three plates and mug were empty—I'd hardly noticed I was eating—I'd narrowed down Numero Uno's identity to a few possibilities. I was pretty sure Numero Dos was one of two people. Tres was a little more overt, probably a drug cartel boss I'd actually read about in the papers. He seemed like the type to leave the unsubtle hint of a disembodied finger.

Clarice had Siete, Ocho and Nueve nailed down. I checked my watch. The middle of the group would have to wait.

"Gotta go," I said, laying a couple crisp twenties from my ATM raid the other day on the table. "This ought to cover it since the waitress won't be back with our bill for a week."

We packed our things and fled, smiling guiltily at the clumps of people waiting restlessly in the restaurant's small foyer. I'm not sure I could have scarfed my food any faster, though.

Butterflies or the consequence of the reams of grease I'd consumed? Regardless, the hard knot in my stomach grew bigger the closer we got to the rendezvous point.

Clarice peered at the driving instructions and barked commands. Turned out the location I'd selected was the site of two fast food establishments of the non-playland variety and a green-space rest stop next to the freeway.

I parked facing a row of battered picnic tables, a few spaces away from an empty minivan with two training wheel equipped bicycles strapped to the liftgate. It was far too cold for enjoyable outdoor dining. A semitruck sat idling at the far end of the parking lot, its exhaust brownish-gray.

Wind gusts whipped a couple paper food wrappers around the pickup, and one got stuck in a windshield wiper. It crinkled against the glass for a few seconds before escaping.

"We drove four hours for this?" Clarice grumbled.

I craned my neck around and didn't see a single person not in a moving vehicle zipping down the freeway. "Not too many witnesses." Of course, the staff and customers in the taco and sub sandwich joints might glance out the windows, but I had to count on their being hungry or busy enough to not be curious.

Clarice shivered. "How long?"

I checked my watch. Then I pulled one of the prepaid phones from my tote and checked it for messages, but there were none. I shook my head. "Depends on customs."

Clarice's lips pinched into a tight bundle of wrinkles, but she spared me a comment.

A white, unmarked step van with British Columbia plates puttered along the access road, the turn signal blinking conscientiously. At the sight of the wide brown face of the man behind the wheel, my tension—well, most of it—slipped away. I hopped out of the pickup and waved.

He parked next to us, on the side away from the minivan. His door slammed, and I met him at the back of the step van.

"Any trouble?"

"Nora." A huge smile creased his face, and he engulfed me in a bear hug. "First things first. Are you all right?" He held me by the shoulders at arm's length and studied me.

His black hair was streaked with more gray than last time I'd seen him, but the black eyes were the same— intense and worried.

"I'm going to take the Fifth on that," I whispered, "as I'm sure you know by my request." I blinked back welling tears. "But is it ever good to see you." I gave him another squeeze around his sturdy midsection.

Art Williams, in spite of his commonplace English name, is a First Nations elder. He directs social services for the collection of tribes in his jurisdiction. I first met him in Prince George while investigating a range of health initiatives the tribes were starting to implement. I was hoping to share their successful measures with medical facilities Skip's foundation supports in Africa. I came away from those few days with a whole host of great ideas and a friend for life in Art. He worked tirelessly to help his people—and now, to help me.

"Well, if it isn't Clarice." Art grabbed Clarice for a bear hug too, which she tolerated stiffly. He cast one extra glance over the top of her head, where her hair used to be, but maintained remarkable stoicism.

Then he turned back to me. "I will want answers," he said in a low voice, "but I understand time is of the essence. With regard to your enquiry—only the usual list of complacent questions at the border and a quick peek at the cargo. But I don't know if my ticker could survive that again." He patted his chest with one hand and unlatched the roll-up rear door of the step van with the other. "Our Women's and Children's Relief Fund is going to support a free vision and dental clinic with part of your donation. We have yet to figure out what to do with the rest." He shook his head. "The grand total, of what showed up in all our accounts, blew our minds, Nora."

I grinned. "My pleasure—and Skip's."

Art climbed into the back of the van and hefted a plastic bag. "Bucket brigade style? They're forty pounds apiece." He set the bag into my waiting arms.

Clarice unlatched the pickup's tailgate and tipped her upper half over it, wriggling and scrambling with her legs in the air. She would have been horrified if she knew how ridiculous she looked, so I struggled to suppress my giggling. She certainly wouldn't have appreciated a boost. Besides, I had my hands full. She finally scootched her belly and then her hips onto the truck bed and pushed up onto her knees.

"You're really getting the hang of this country living thing," I said.

"Shut up." She grabbed my bag, dropped it with a surprised ooof, then pushed it up against the cab. "Get a move on, girl."

I shifted into autopilot and lost count of the bags I transferred. In fact, I purposely tried to disengage my brain from my body so I didn't get so many stop-you're-killing-me signals. I doubted my poor, underused muscles would let me walk tomorrow.

Somewhere mid-stream, the minivan family strolled out of the taco joint, clambered into their vehicle and drove off without giving us a second glance. Several other travelers took brief respites in the parking lot too, but none seemed to take particular notice of us. Maybe black market deals were a common occurrence. Maybe people knew better than to ask.

Art took care of strapping our load, for which I was grateful. The piled layers of bags blocked all but the top few inches of the cab's rear window. Bertha's back tires bulged, and I didn't have much faith in the integrity of her shock absorbers.

Art shared a skeptical look with me. "Good luck. Drive slow."

"That part won't be difficult." I leaned closer to him. "I know this,"—I waved a hand toward the overburdened pickup—"what I asked of you, is illegal. Thank you," I whispered.

Art slipped a warm hand under my elbow. "Only for you, Nora, given your extreme circumstances. I don't want anything to happen to you. Promise you'll stay in touch?"

I nodded.

"It'll be dark in another hour—hour and a half." Clarice announced.

Art squeezed my arm. "Go. Text me when you're safely home. I won't be able to sleep until you do."

I laid a hand on his cheek. "You're a good man, Art Williams."

"Don't I know it." He smiled again, but the expression didn't erase the worry from his eyes.

CHAPTER 19

Art took the northbound on-ramp while Clarice and I chugged up the southbound entrance to I-5, Bertha's springs groaning. No question we were an eyesore, and we garnered plenty of irritated glances as drivers slammed on their brakes behind us then sped past as soon as possible.

"Am I supposed to believe those bags are full of wood pellets like the labels say?" Clarice asked.

She was becoming peskier than a four-year-old in the *why?* stage. "They're a free trade product under NAFTA," I answered.

Clarice snorted. "I wasn't born yesterday."

"I didn't think you were."

Clarice stewed in silence as dusk descended. The pickup was making new noises which put me in a state of high alert. I compulsively checked the mirrors to see if any bags had slipped. If we lost even one, it might trigger an investigation that would be disastrous for Art as well as Clarice and me.

While all the rural parts of the state I'd seen so far were about trees, the Seattle metro area was all about traffic, which backed up fast and for miles. We were bookended in the slow lane—rolling, stopping, rolling, stopping. I read the political smorgasbord of bumper stickers on the car in front of us twenty times. My toes cramped from fluctuating pressure on the clutch and gas pedals.

I fiddled with knobs until the headlamps came on. In the dim glow of the dashboard light, the fuel gauge needle vibrated in the red zone.

"I need an exit with a gas station," I said. "Soon."

Clarice peered through the windshield, reading aloud all the signs, relevant or not.

I think I held my breath until the bright Texaco sign came into view. Just as I pulled in next to the pumps, one of my phones rang.

"Art," Clarice whispered hoarsely. "He got caught."

"He doesn't have the incriminating evidence anymore. We do." I finally found the phone that was lit up. "Besides, wrong phone."

I plastered a fake smile on my face, even though the caller couldn't see me, and answered. "Hi, Mom."

Beside me, Clarice snorted, but I refused to look at her.

"It's your lucky day," Mom piped.

"I sure hope so."

"Josh Freeney. He's your disgraced FBI agent."

"You're sure?" I scrambled for some paper and a pencil, but Clarice beat me to it, nudging them into my free hand.

"Of course I am. His wife goes to yoga with my massage therapist's fiancé's mother. The poor woman was in tears and couldn't finish her session. She's considering divorce."

At least she knew where her husband was, which was one step ahead of me.

"You're amazing," I said.

"Yes, honey. Now for your other request. I couldn't tell if the florist's clerk was inherently obstinate or just obtuse. He hemmed and hawed but finally gave me the email address used for your order's confirmation. What a lovely bouquet," Mom gushed. "Did you know it cost almost three hundred dollars, not including delivery?"

"The email address?" I tried to keep irritation from creeping into my voice.

"Oh yes." Mom spelled out the address, and I scribbled it down.

A meaningless combination of letters and numbers, not someone's personal account. The domain extension was Australian. Email accounts can be forwarded and rerouted endlessly, so I didn't put too much stock in the location. Probably meant to be a diversion, which also meant I'd be wasting any more time spent trying to track it down.

But the idea reinforced my hope that Skip was still alive. It also escalated the gnawing feeling that he was leaving me alone to clean up his mess while he bailed out. Skip—if it was Skip—was blowing money on roses while I resorted to illegal activity to support myself and the boys' camp I was placing in danger.

If he was alive—where was he? One hardly sends three-hundred-dollar flower arrangements from a kidnapper's concrete cell while subsisting on gruel and water.

A knuckle rapped hard on my window, and I jumped.

A haggard, middle-aged man in a khaki uniform stood next to the truck, his badge shiny under the gas station's florescent lights.

"Uh-oh." Clarice's face wrinkled into a ghastly approximation of a smile as she nodded to the officer through the window. "Nora," she hissed through immobile lips, "do something."

"Hang on," I blurted to Mom. I wrestled with the window's crank handle until I got it down halfway.

"Evening." The officer tipped his head. "Where are you ladies headed?"

"Home." My mouth was still open, although I didn't know what else to add to that statement without implicating myself, when a tinny voice screeched from the phone in my lap.

It was a good thing we couldn't make out Mom's words, although her agitated, high-pitched tone conveyed enough meaning.

"My mother," I said. "Didn't want to drive and talk at the same time. Oh, and we need gas."

Clarice surreptitiously pinched me in the side—hard.

I held up the phone. "Would you like to tell my mother I'm not in trouble?"

The officer cracked a reluctant grin. "Nope. You have a heavy load here. Good job securing it."

The tightness in my chest eased. "Thank you." I tried fluttering my eyelashes.

That made him reach for his gun.

Whew—I exhaled—he was just resting his hands on his hips, arms akimbo.

"You have a brake light out." He said it wearily, as if it was the fourteenth negligent brake light of his shift, and he wished people would just get it together so he could stop repeating himself.

"Really?" Not exactly a surprise—yet another item in a long list of things wrong with Bertha. I tried to make my face ditzy blank. "Which one?"

"Left. Driver's side."

"Thanks for telling me. I'll get it fixed right away."

He frowned down Bertha's entire length, then brought his gaze back to my window. "Drive safe."

"Yes, sir." My sincerity was overwhelming. That was exactly what I planned to do.

Why do cops walk so slowly? Clarice and I watched him stroll to his cruiser and lean against the door's logo, apparently content to take a break while talking on the radio through his open window.

The tinny tirade hadn't stopped. Clarice reached over and punched the end call button on my phone, and the screen went dark.

"Good grief," she muttered. "How long was he back there?"

"No idea. I can't see directly behind us because of the load."

"Pump the gas. Let's get out of here."

I couldn't have agreed with her more.

~oOo~

"I hate to tell you this," I said as we bounced over the rutted track toward the mansion, "but we have to unload the truck tonight. I don't want to keep Bertha out past her curfew. I expect Walt will need her tomorrow."

Clarice had latched onto the seat with both hands to avoid levitating. Her technique wasn't entirely successful. "Next time you go on an adventure—" she paused as her internal organs resettled after a big bump, "remind me not to tag along."

"Stop complaining," I said through clenched teeth. "We could have blown a muffler or a drive train or a carburetor or—or worse." I was actually elated. The mission had been accomplished, and we hadn't been arrested.

"There's nothing worse. Besides I'm talking about the fact that my arms and legs are about to fall off from the first loading."

I'd forgotten about our previous exertion since all my energy had been directed toward fighting Bertha's tendency to drift for the past several hours. My muscles had morphed into rigid bands, operating of their own accord. Bertha had held together, but I had to admit Clarice was right. I wasn't sure my body would do the same once I let go of the steering wheel.

"The question is, where to put them?" I couldn't afford to let my mind be distracted by my body's condition.

"Not in the kitchen," Clarice said in a tone that was not to be argued with. "I'm assuming, even if it is just wood pellets, that you don't want them out in the open?"

"Correct."

"There's a coal chute around back, near where Bertha was parked this morning."

I shot her a surprised glance.

"Although I am not yet older than dirt, I do recognize a coal chute when I see one."

I dropped Clarice at the kitchen door so she could thread through the mansion's basement, flipping on light switches along the way, and unlock the door to the room with the coal chute. I drove around and shone Bertha's weak headlamps at the outside of that same door until it opened. Clarice stood in sight of my side mirror and directed me with sweeping arm gestures as I backed old Bertha as close to the chute as possible.

"Hey," she said as I climbed out of the pickup, "did you know your left brake light is out?"

Clarice propped open the hatch and retreated to the bottom of the chute. I shoved bags through the opening one at a time. With gravity doing most of the work, the task was appreciably easier than the first time. There was no need to make a tidy stack, so Clarice managed bottlenecks at the downhill end by kicking bags out of the way.

"In spite of our now ample fuel source," she shouted through the hole, "I'm running on fumes. Breakfast was too long ago. How many more bags?"

"Last one," I grunted, heaving the bag onto the slide.

My aim must have deteriorated, because the bag shot over the shallow bumper at the edge of the chute and fell to the floor, spilling its contents in a golden stream.

Clarice scowled and bent over, snatching up several of the green packets that had escaped along with the wood pellets. She riffled the edge of one of the packets. "Nora?"

I sighed. "You said you'd find out eventually. Now you know."

"Undeclared?"

"I'm not in a position to use banking services just now. Art, out of the goodness of his heart, returned a fraction of the donations the foundation deposited in their accounts. And looks like he did it in U.S. currency. God bless that man."

"Whatchya doing?" The bright voice was followed by a brighter set of blue eyes popping into the square of light shining through the coal chute door. Eli wedged in beside me and stared down at Clarice.

I didn't know she could move so fast. Her fists with the money disappeared behind her back and she side-shuffled, trying to block the rest of the spill on the floor from his view.

"Eli." My reaction was a split-second behind Clarice's. I grabbed his shoulder and pulled him away from the chute, too roughly. "What are *you* doing? I thought you were grounded to the bunkhouse."

"Just one day." He wriggled out of my grasp, his face pinched.

I straightened and rubbed my forehead. "Boys your age should be in bed by now."

His shoulders lifted in a defensive, apologetic gesture, shrinking his neck as well as his voice. "Dwayne told me to come."

"You were with Dwayne now, tonight?"

He nodded vigorously. "I took him dinner. I'm supposed to get you."

My heart started hammering. This did not bode well. "Why?"

"He found another man who's not supposed to be here."

"What's this?" Clarice grunted from the top of the basement stairs. She slammed the door behind her, then reached over and secured the coal chute hatch.

"Right now?" I squeaked.

Eli nodded again. "Dwayne says he can hold the varmint until you get there. What's a varmint?"

Clarice huffed with impatience. "Who's Dwayne?"

"Let's go." I hustled Eli to the pickup's driver's door, picked him up—I was getting good at heaving dead weights around—and thrust him onto the seat. "Scoot over."

I had Bertha in gear before Clarice made it onto her side of the seat and smacked her door closed.

"Hang on," I shouted. We didn't have time for seat belts.

All I could think about was that horrible, rusty old shotgun and what might happen if Dwayne's shaky finger snagged the trigger. And just how long it would take an ambulance to find us out here in the boonies.

CHAPTER 20

The trail Eli led us down felt like a rabbit hole. At least Bertha sat, still rocking on her springs, out on the gravel road as a marker of where we'd taken off on foot. Clarice and I had a rough time, tripping over unseen roots and rocks and each other in the dark. For a fleeting moment, I was envious of the FBI's mega lights for nighttime forest exploration.

Eli kept hold of my sleeve and I maintained contact with Clarice, or we would have been lost for good. A faint yellow glow grew in the distance. Eli darted between branches while Clarice and I crashed through the underbrush. In a way, our noisy trampling comforted me. Dwayne would surely hear us coming and maybe resist the urge to do something foolish with that shotgun.

In the light of a hissing propane lantern, its flame curling hungrily around the wick, Dwayne stood stiffly over a crouching boy. They were in what could best be called the portico of a shack—a shack with a tarp, sheets of plywood, and pieces of rickety wood pallets aesthetic.

I bent at an odd angle, clutching my side and gasping, checking over the people in the scene one more time. No one seemed to be in immediate danger.

Dwayne nodded to me, the shotgun balanced in the relaxed hand at his side.

The boy—maybe he was a young man, hard to tell in the dim light—had his arms wrapped around his legs as though his limbs had minds of their own and he was trying to corral them. He twitched uncontrollably. He sure didn't look like the trusted messenger of an organized crime syndicate. He looked cold.

"Caught him poking around," Dwayne said. "Had this." He nudged a black object with his toe. A small handgun.

"Is it real?" I asked.

"Yep. Piddly .22."

I squatted beside the boy. He blinked fast and flicked his gaze everywhere but at me.

"What's your name?"

Most people can answer that question in a few seconds. He failed to do so.

I leaned closer, and his breathing, already fast, quickened. His hair was thin and flat, and several painful-looking sores ringed his mouth. And then I knew. He wasn't a threat in himself, but his behavior could be irrational and unpredictably violent.

"When was your last hit?"

He shrugged.

"Meth?"

Another shrug.

"What were you doing with the gun?"

"Hunting rabbits." His teeth were broken, and one on the bottom was missing.

Dwayne blew out air in a soft grunt. He wasn't buying the boy's story.

"Where's your family?"

Shrug.

"Are you alone?"

His lips pressed together. I was pretty sure that was a yes.

"Do you have a place to sleep?"

A quick glance over his shoulder, which I took as a negative answer.

"Are you hungry?"

Direct eye contact for a fleeting moment.

I rose to my feet. The look on Clarice's face told me she knew too. You can't walk the streets of San Francisco, even as a casual observer, and not know.

"We need Walt," I said. "Dwayne, if it's all right?" It was his house, after all, the secrecy of which he'd guarded carefully.

Dwayne nodded.

Eli's huge eyes turned to me, studying my face, as though seeking the assurance of a responsible party. I expected, with his background, he may have seen something like this before. As much as I hated the idea of using an eight-year-old as a messenger in the dark, in the woods, with unknown crazies roaming about, Eli had proven his adeptness at the task. "Please?" I whispered.

He disappeared from the circle of light cast by the propane lamp.

"Dwayne, this is my good friend, Clarice Wheaton."

They exchanged stiff nods. We were a taciturn bunch.

"Um, Clarice, would you take custody of the handgun? Dwayne, do you have a couple spare blankets?"

"Inside." Dwayne shuffled a few steps sideways to give Clarice room to pick up the gun while still keeping his stern gaze fixed on the intruder.

The door to Dwayne's shack was open a few inches. I pushed on the flimsy wood and ducked inside. The house was a clump of small rooms cobbled together, but with distinct functions. The first room was a combination sitting and cooking space. Beyond that was a closet-sized addition with a cot and a few pegs on the walls.

Another room looked like storage with a jumble of empty crates, tubing, and metal tubs. Vats—that would be the correct term. I wasn't an expert on hooch-making, but they sure looked like moonshine supplies. I suppose if you're drinking straight alcohol then sanitation isn't an issue.

Dwayne—all two times I'd seen him—had never appeared intoxicated. Shaky, yes, but I attributed that to old age. He was entirely lucid.

I slipped into the bedroom. I doubted the boy would mind, but the rumpled blankets on the cot didn't smell as though they'd been washed in a while. I knelt and peered under the cot in case Dwayne had a stash of spare bedding. He didn't seem to have spare much of anything, but it was worth a look.

I pulled out a bulging rucksack and opened the flap. For the second time that day, I was staring at bundles of cash.

How long had it been since I'd slept? I wiped my eyes and pinched a packet of the money. It was real. But old, grungy bills, exactly the wadded-up-then-flattened notes you'd expect to pass from one hillbilly hand to another—not like the crisp, fresh cotton/linen paper from the bank packs that Clarice had whipped behind her back earlier.

I replaced the money, cinched the bag even tighter and shoved it under the cot until it bumped the outer wall. Was distilling really that lucrative? And yet Dwayne stole potatoes from growing boys. I'd have to talk to him about his operating procedures—later.

I scooped the bedding off the cot and hurried outside. The boy was rocking now, unsteady on his heels, still hunkered on the mud-caked wood planks. I knelt beside him and draped the blankets over his shoulders. His next several hours would be horrible.

I knew better than to touch him, but I sat close to him with my back against the front of Dwayne's shack and my legs outstretched. The boy needed to know that I wouldn't desert him, that help was coming, that he'd get through the night.

Dwayne relaxed his stance and stuffed the shotgun in the crook of his elbow. The barrel ended up aimed at the roof over my head, but at least his finger was nowhere near the trigger. Clarice tipped up a chunk of split wood and slowly lowered herself onto the impromptu seat with a groan.

About ten million snatches of thoughts raced through my mind, but the only one that stuck and repeated was that I could have skipped the trip to Bellingham and just asked Dwayne for a loan—if I'd known. Of course, it would have had to be on generous terms because without the trip to Bellingham I'd never have been able to repay him.

It seemed like forever—I might have dozed—and my toes grew numb inside my boots. The boy beside me kept up his interminable rocking.

"I'm Nora," I finally said, my voice echoing in the silence. Maybe he'd trust me with his name if he knew mine.

But his eyes were blank and distant.

"And I'm Santa Claus," Clarice muttered.

Dwayne chuckled. "You'd need my beard for that."

"No question you have a magnificent specimen," Clarice retorted, "but I'll pass." She seemed about to topple off her stump seat. She had to be exhausted beyond consciousness—I knew I was.

"You still wearing the whistle?" Dwayne asked.

I placed my hand over the bump hanging below my collarbone. "Yes."

Dwayne nodded. "Good idea."

Eli arrived with Walt in tow. I exhaled—I hadn't realized I'd been holding my breath, relieved only by shallow pants, until my lungs let go. Walt would know what to do.

He strode up to Dwayne, his hand outstretched. "Heard you found him."

"Yep." Dwayne pumped Walt's hand.

"Poaching?"

"Claims so. I have my doubts."

Walt came and knelt in front of the boy and me. His left hand landed on my knee with a gentle squeeze. "Nora." His gaze was questioning, but I just shook my head.

"Help me get him up."

The boy weighed next to nothing and was as wobbly as a newborn colt. I supported him with an arm around his middle while Walt gripped his shoulders with both hands.

The timbre of Walt's voice changed, became compelling. "Have any on you?"

The boy shook his head.

"I'm going to check your pockets." Walt didn't wait for the boy's permission and frisked him thoroughly. When he was satisfied the boy was telling the truth—at least about current drug possession—he straightened. "Fair enough. You can stay with us tonight. We'll figure out what to do in the morning."

I leaned close to Walt and whispered, "Thank you. I know this wasn't your first choice of things to do tonight. Wasn't mine either." I pulled the keys out of my pocket and pressed them into his hand. "Take Bertha." He didn't exhibit even the slightest twitch at the fact that I'd named his truck. "I have Skip's clothes. They'll be too big, but they're something."

"In the morning." Walt's lips curved into a faint, sad smile. "I guess we have a lot to talk about."

I returned Dwayne's blankets, and we trooped through the woods to the potholed track. The man and men-to-be climbed into Bertha for the drive to safety and warm beds. Clarice and I turned the other direction and prepared our minds for a moonlit trudge.

"If I may ask again, who, exactly, is Dwayne?" Clarice said, her breath rising in steam puffs timed with her footfalls.

"Mayfield's resident hermit and purveyor of fine spirits. Oh, and he has a sack of money under his cot."

"You mean like our sacks of money?" Clarice snorted. "Isn't that just dandy—sacks of money for everyone." After a few minutes, she added, "Maybe *he's* Santa Claus. Do you think we're ever going to wake up from this dream?"

"I sure hope so."

My phone rang. I should say *one* of my phones rang. I had to set my bag in the middle of the road and paw through it to find the correct culprit. Which reminded me that I still needed to text Art. I slung the bag back over my shoulder, answered the ringing phone and started a text on the phone dedicated to Art.

"Heard you had a visitor," Matt said.

"Mmhmm." I thumbed buttons. *Safely home &—*

"Any more excitement today?" Matt asked.

"Nope," I lied. It wasn't the kind of excitement he needed to know about.

—unpacked.

I tripped over a rock and nearly went sprawling. Clarice wrenched my arm to keep me from having a technological disaster on the gravel.

I rehitched my purse and tuned back in to the phone where Matt was saying, "What was that?" with a panicked edge to his voice.

"Just me being clumsy."

Clarice pulled the texting phone from my grasp and hit send.

"Tell him thank you," I whispered to her, stabbing a forefinger at the phone in her hand.

"What for?" Matt asked.

"Oh, uh, sending Violet and the team. Any results?"

"Not yet on your visitor. DNA results take several days even if they're rushed. However, we do know who the fingers belonged to."

"Past tense." I glanced at Clarice, but she was keying furiously, carrying on a text conversation with Art.

"Yeah. The rest of him washed up near the San Leandro Marina early this morning."

I froze in my tracks. Clarice maintained momentum for a few steps then turned back, her face freakishly underlit by the phone's screen.

"His name?"

"Alejandro Vicente Rojas. A capo of sorts in the main San Francisco area drug distribution ring. Sinaloa connections. He was known to function as the banker or bookkeeper for the group."

"And he was killed for his error in judgment in trusting my husband."

"That'd be my guess too."

"How many fingers was he missing?"

"Just the two."

"Dead before or after the fingers were removed?"

"The ME hasn't had a chance to make that determination yet."

"He's not on the list of unreimbursed clients."

"What list?"

I scowled. Had he forgotten Skip's journal? I wasn't in the mood to remind him. "What about Leroy?"

"Full of bluster, but deflated fast. He claims he knew something fishy was going on, maybe even participated in some of it, but has no familiarity with the bones of the operation. We've tried scaring it out of him in every legal way possible. I'm beginning to think he's one of the few people on the planet who actually does know less than he's willing to admit to. And he's lawyered up, so we're finished with him for now."

"You didn't let him go?" I hollered, startling a small creature that crashed through the brush to my left.

Clarice gripped my elbow, and I got the message. I should not be yelling in the woods tonight, of all nights. Stealth was our preferred mode, all things considered.

"Course not." Matt sounded disgruntled. "The judge agreed Leroy's attempt to bribe a flight crew made his promise to be available for the next hearing questionable, so she denied bail. Leroy's warming a cell and will be for a while."

"So we're waiting again." I resumed walking, Clarice falling into step beside me.

"Afraid so. We'll work the homicide angle with the San Leandro police, but these kinds of message-sending murders aren't that uncommon, especially in organized crime and drug circles. One of many."

"This one affects me."

"Noted. You might want to install new locks." Matt hung up.

I exhaled hard, but it did nothing to release my frustration.

"On a cheerful note," Clarice said, "Art recrossed the border without difficulty and is home. Says Myrna is making traditional flatbread and venison stew and we should come for dinner."

"I wish. The FBI might be the long arm of the law, but they sure aren't making progress fast enough to suit me."

"I imagine with all the terrorists and human traffickers and Coach luggage counterfeiters and whatnot running around that we're pretty low on their priority list." Clarice linked her arm through mine. "I might know a few things that would help Leroy pick details out of his fuzzy memory. Or I could just call his wife."

CHAPTER 21

There's nothing like a pile of stolen cash in the basement, the weight-lifting workout of the decade, the dismembered body of a revenge killing, and a desperate drug addict wandering loose on your property to ruin a girl's beauty sleep. Walt didn't look any better than I did.

"Rough night?" I asked as I reached to flick the stove knob to heat water for Matt's French press. I stretched slowly and deliberately, wincing only when my back was turned to Walt. An agonizing burn spasmed all of my muscles in unison every time I moved.

Clarice had yet to make an appearance, and I was glad one of us was able to rest.

Walt sat at the kitchen table and scrubbed his few days' beard growth with a calloused hand. "He crashed about two hours ago. Dill's sitting with him now."

"Did you?" I smeared peanut butter on a slice of bread.

"What?"

"Sleep?"

Walt shook his head. "Been a long time since I've stayed with someone who's tweaking. Pretty mild case, really."

"Did you find out his name?"

"He mumbled some stuff. I think it's Bodie." Walt accepted a sandwich dripping with honey. I slid a paper towel in front of him as a plate and napkin all in one. My housekeeping standards had dropped considerably.

I returned to the sticky implements to make a sandwich for myself. "That's an unusual name."

"There's a family about ten miles out, in the Dark Divide." Walt tipped his head in the direction—maybe east? "The Ramsay family. Everything about them is unusual. If he's one of theirs—and I think he is—I can't in good conscience send him back."

Walt always seems to have an underpinning of worry, but as his eyes searched mine, I realized this was more intense than usual.

"How bad?" I couldn't sit without groaning, so I leaned against the counter and tore off a corner of my sandwich.

"Cultish. The father's completely domineering and has bizarre ideas about end times. They've taken survivalism to an extreme level. No one's sure how many kids they have, but some of them haven't been seen in years, in particular two girls."

The peanut butter stuck in my mouth, and I fought to swallow. "Bodie stays. Absolutely." I wanted to snatch all his siblings, too, and spirit them to safety. "Can we do that, legally?"

"He may be close to eighteen. I doubt he has a birth certificate. When he's coherent, I'll see what information I can get out of him."

"Where would he get drugs?"

"The family might be making it. Meth's pretty easy to cook."

The forest was full of illicit commerce—moonshine, methamphetamine—an entire black market under cover of rolling, wooded hills with neighbors spaced so widely you could get away with anything. All we were missing were anarchists. I shuddered at the thought.

"They sell it?" I asked.

Walt wiped his fingers on the paper towel. "I suspect that's how they support themselves."

"Another fugitive," I whispered.

"You mean Mayfield's become a haven for a bunch of misfits?" Walt actually grinned. "She always has been. We're just restoring her original purpose."

"My two favorite people," Clarice announced from the doorway. She strode into the room and plunked something heavy and metallic on the table—hair clippers. "I haven't seen all your boys yet, Walt, but the ones I have seen are shaggy about the ears. I'm a good hand with these—" she wiggled the clippers, "as you may have just noticed, so bring them over this afternoon and we'll have a barbering session."

I grabbed the handle of Skip's wheeled suitcase which I had repacked and propelled it toward Walt. "And these clothes, for whomever they fit best."

Walt's glance darted from the top of Clarice's head to me and back again, but he had the grace not to comment on her makeover. He rose slowly, brushing crumbs off the table with the crumpled paper towel. "I guess that's what we get for letting girls move in. You're going to make us clean up." But his eyes were sparkling.

I beamed at him and vowed to myself to do whatever I could to ease his heavy-heartedness.

Walt opened the kitchen door and jostled the suitcase over the threshold. Then he turned back. "You know you can't burn wood pellets in a regular fireplace, right? Well, you can, but it's dangerous. They burn super hot. I could weld you a contraption—a fireplace insert that would hold the pellets and allow for even oxygen supply. I need to clean the chimney before you use it, too."

"Really?" I managed.

Walt nodded, his eyes narrowed.

"Thanks," I whispered. My voice had deserted me.

When the door clicked closed behind Walt, Clarice whooshed as though her lungs had been punctured. "How much did Eli see?"

"And how much did he tell?" I added.

~oOo~

I placed a call to my new friend Josh Freeney, another person whose life had been turned upside down by Skip, and left a message. I wasn't surprised that he wasn't answering his phone. I wouldn't be either, in his shoes. Clarice had a long, juicy chat with Leroy Hardiman's wife, Josie.

Our cajoling and sleuthing had turned long-distance, but in my current condition, I much preferred a day of a phone pressed to my ear versus a day rattling down the highway in Bertha.

Clarice sat, twiddling with her phone, after the call with Josie ended.

"Talk to me," I said.

Clarice sighed. "While she had numerous tales of his personal infidelity, she didn't present her husband as particularly intelligent."

"Not surprising. I could tell from across the room that she's furious. She's not likely to be in a mood to compliment him."

"But maybe Skip selected Leroy as his gopher for his questionable morality to start with. Hen-pecked," Clarice grumbled. "Does exactly what his wife tells him to do, so I suspect he acquiesced to Skip too. Much as I hate to admit it, maybe he doesn't really know anything."

"Except how to call a lawyer."

"Oh yes. He's very good at that."

"Makes sense. Skip kept the journal. Skip handled the accounts. Skip claimed financial bamboozlement when he clearly had an extremely organized and detailed accounting system." I poured the dregs of the coffee into my mug and set the French press in the sink. My wedding ring still rested on the window sill, dull in the gray morning light. I balanced it in my palm for a minute and returned it to banishment. "I guess I'm finally ready to admit Skip lied—he lied a whole lot."

"Kiddo, I'm sorry." Clarice stood and slipped an arm around my waist, pulling me in for a hug. "But if we assume everything he said is false until proven true, we might make more progress."

I nodded, a tear sliding down my cheek. "And what are the odds that I never receive a ransom phone call?"

"You know what I want to do?" Clarice said abruptly. "Now that we're wealthy? Feed those boys. How long do you think it's been since they've had a proper Christmas dinner? We need to go shopping."

"Christmas is a couple weeks away yet."

"I need to get a few practice rounds in first."

And so we went shopping—since shopping solves everything, or at least somehow makes the inevitable more tolerable. Actually, I knew what Clarice was doing—there was less chance of my slipping into morose solitude and depression if she kept me hopping—and I was grateful for her bustle.

~oOo~

We returned from town with the station wagon loaded to the gills and a fair bit of gossip from Etherea about the Ramsay family, including a rough guess at Bodie's age which matched Walt's estimate. I'm sure she suspected why we asked, but she seemed more than happy to pass along all the details in her possession, especially after I settled our tab and paid cash for our newest purchases.

I had a few nervous flutters in my stomach about my law of separation being violated by our hosting Walt and all the boys at the mansion, but I shoved them away. It was hard not to want to toast our successful run toward the border for cash, even if Clarice and I couldn't tell anyone why we were celebrating.

Walt arrived in the early afternoon, herding his reluctant flock. He must have warned them what was coming. We set up an assembly line on the patio, complete with kitchen chairs, bed sheets, clothespins, and an extension cord Clarice found in the basement.

The younger boys submitted somewhat willingly, especially when I let them pick out yarn for their new hats. It would be a terrific way to learn all their names, I realized, as I made a list and noted their favorite colors.

But the older boys had a few determined opinions about their future appearance, and when Thomas announced his intention to have dreadlocks, Clarice rolled her eyes and stomped into the kitchen. I scowled at his mischievous smirk and decided to pull out the big guns.

"Nora, how are you?" Sidonie panted with a kind of breathless happiness as if I'd caught her in the middle of a physically demanding but enjoyable task. Given her size, just getting to the phone probably required planning.

"Do you know anything about hair? Boys' hair in particular?"

She must have sensed my desperation, because Sidonie said curtly, "We'll be right there," and hung up.

"You're in for it now," I muttered to Thomas, but he just settled lower in the chair with a satisfied glint in his eyes and laced his fingers over his skinny middle.

Amazing smells were starting to waft from the kitchen—cinnamon, yeasty warmth, pot roast, and if I wasn't mistaken, lemon. Clarice had set several of the boys to food preparation jobs after she'd supervised their hand washing efforts. The rest lounged around loose-jointed, forming a constantly morphing peanut gallery for the temporary salon on the patio or getting underfoot in the kitchen as only boys can do, poking each other, teasing, talking loudly, and showing off a little.

Bodie loitered apart from any groups, so weak he couldn't seem to stand upright but leaned against the wall, with black circles under his eyes, his narrow shoulders hunched inside one of Skip's jackets. The noise and activity seemed to overwhelm him. Clarice slipped him an apple which he devoured in just a few bites.

The Gonzales family—all five of them—arrived in their beat-up blue pickup which could have been Bertha's twin. I was learning that nobody wasted money on nice vehicles in May County because the roads wreaked havoc on their chassis in short order. Sidonie propped open her door and slid out, cradling her belly with both arms on the descent.

Walt hurried over to offer assistance, but instead Sidonie turned, hoisted a giant, foil-covered casserole dish off the seat and thrust it into his hands. Hank came around the cab with CeCe in his arms. The men, equally laden, nodded to each other.

Sidonie pulled a massive, hot-fuchsia, faux alligator carryall from the pickup's floorboard and hitched the straps over her shoulder. "Where's the fire?"

I pointed at Thomas, whose smug look had been replaced with a sudden nervous shiftiness. Sidonie marched straight up to him and stood, her belly inches from his shoulder, scrutinizing his budding afro. She made clucking noises and started prodding his scalp while Thomas slouched even lower.

I spun to hide my grin and found Walt turning a pretty shade of pink from trying not to laugh himself. I peeked under the foil—tamales!—and relieved him of the casserole dish. Clarice made room for the tamales in the warming oven.

I finished trimming the hair of the boys who didn't need Sidonie's expertise and returned to the warm, steamy kitchen. The boys had settled down and were hovering closer and closer to the table, motivated by the increasingly good swirl of odors in the large, but currently cramped room. I waded through them and found Walt and Hank in a corner, deep in quiet conversation.

CeCe clung to her dad's side and peeked up at me shyly. Eli knelt beside her, trying to interest her in a bracelet made of knotted string and a few tiny pinecones. I gave him an encouraging wink. In a few minutes, I was pretty sure he'd win her over.

The men paused at my approach.

"Thank you for coming," I said to Hank.

His dark eyes were serious but kind. He was not the sort of man who smiled often, and he spoke even less. But when he did smile, his whole face lit up, and I knew instantly why Sidonie had fallen in love with him. They were perfect opposites. "Glad to." He rested his hand on CeCe's head, a gentle caress.

I touched Walt's shoulder. "It's your turn."

"For what?"

I lifted my eyes to his stocking cap, from under which poked shaggy tufts of hair.

Walt grimaced. "I was hoping to avoid that."

"To what good purpose?" I grinned. "Come on. Set an example, even if you are last."

Walt and Thomas, his dreads coming along nicely under Sidonie's deft twisting and gelling, shared a look of commiseration as Walt took a seat on the spare chair.

I pulled off Walt's hat and his hair stood on end in a startling display of static electricity. I tried to pat it down, giggling. "Any preferences?"

"Shave it off," Walt muttered.

"You sure? You'll be cold." I dropped his hat in his lap and clipped on his cape.

"Maybe you'll knit me a new, warmer hat. This one has holes."

"Maybe." I rested a hand on the back of his neck, gently pushing his head forward and down. "No wiggling."

Walt relaxed under my touch as I ran the clippers in even lines across his scalp. It'd been the same with all the boys—initial awkward stiffness, then pliancy. It just feels really good to have someone massaging your head. Women know this—I think it's our main motivator for frequent salon visits. Guys don't have the same excuse for luxurious attention.

I wondered about all these boys, being raised by a man, with no women in their lives. They were missing out on mom hugs and cuddles—and swats. The little touches you give when you walk by, the tender reassurances, or to emphasize something you just said. They were hungry for caresses, even though they'd never admit it—that and good cooking, apparently.

At orphanages around the globe it was always the same—the kids couldn't be snuggled enough. They scrambled for places on my lap, and if that was full, they draped on me with their arms wrapped around my neck. If we were walking, they insisted on holding my hands, as though the physical contact ensured I wouldn't disappear. Too many adults had already failed them—it was what they expected and feared. The world is full of starving kids—in more than one way.

"Longer on top?" I asked.

"Whatever you want," Walt murmured.

"A dangerous offer."

He grunted, but didn't resist as I tipped his head for a better angle.

I finished and stood frowning in front of him, trying to brush the longer section into some semblance of a part. "Better than a crew cut—maybe."

"It'll do." Walt pulled on his old hat, stretching it down to cover the tops of his ears, and stood. But he flashed a mischievous grin. "Thanks, Nora."

Only Thomas was brave enough for dreads, but Sidonie also performed one set of short cornrow braids and several faux hawks. She drew the line at outright mohawks. She said they were beneath her dignity.

And then we feasted. There wasn't room at the table for all of us, so we reserved those spaces for our guests, the Gonzales family. CeCe sat on her knees and shoveled in tamales with an earnestness that matched the boys'.

I spent a lot of time moving between clusters of happy boys seated on the floor, dropping scoopfuls of second and third and fourth helpings of mashed potatoes, roast beef, butternut squash and Waldorf salad onto proffered paper plates. Bodie ate enough to fill two linebackers. It was the first time most of the boys had tasted tamales, and the contents of the casserole dish evaporated.

It was a good thing Clarice had prepared two huge pans of desserts—peach cobbler and cherry crisp, or we might have had a few hungry boys left over. I was astounded at all the empty dishes lining the counters. We were going to have to adjust our quantity planning for future meals.

I took my bowl of crisp and melting vanilla ice cream outside to catch my breath and cool off. I was sweaty from all the activity and the cramped conditions in the kitchen.

But I wouldn't have it any other way. This was the closest to a real family gathering that I'd had in a very long time, and certainly more joyful than any since my dad was diagnosed with Alzheimer's. As an only child, I'd missed out on the fun—and frustration—of siblings, the good-natured and not-so-good-natured jostling and sharing. I smiled and leaned against the brick wall under the porch light, listening to the happy voices inside.

I like my à la mode a little soupy, so I twirled my spoon, watching the white creaminess ooze amid the cherries and crumbly topping. I wondered how many decades it had been since Dwayne had experienced a family dinner. He deserved a report on Bodie too. I'd hike to his homestead in the morning to issue an invitation for our next meal and have a chat with him. We had several important topics to discuss, not the least of which was his illegal activities on my property. Of course, I was in no position to cast stones in that matter, but I did want to know what other infractions I might need to add to Matt's list for possible prosecution.

There was a soft thud and a warm rush of air from my left. I turned my head just in time to see—nothing.

Rough cloth pressed against my eyes. A hard hand yanked on my jaw, and a dry, scratchy wad was stuffed in my mouth before I had a chance to scream.

CHAPTER 22

I threw my bowl of crisp and heard a grunt as it connected with some soft part of my assailant, or one of his friends. Given the number of hands grabbing and shoving me, there had to be more than one. I forced squeals past the wad in my mouth, but they didn't come out any louder than a mildly irritated chipmunk's.

My arms were jerked in front of me, clamped together, and strapped at the wrists. My fingers went numb almost instantly. I was tugged around the corner, my feet tripping stupidly on the rough ground. Even though I couldn't see, I sensed that I was no longer in the glow cast by the porch light, and I clamped my teeth into the wad to control my violent shivering.

I swung my right foot around, hoping to catch a shin—front, back, sideways. A soft hiss sounded near my ear—a warning—then something bony and hard plowed into my stomach, knocking my breath away, and I was lifted off the ground, middle first.

I flailed as much as I could from my hinged position, glad to still have on my hiking boots with their tough soles. Whoever was carrying me was moving at a full trot, and the hard jouncing felt as though it was cracking my ribs as I struggled to breathe through my nose on each upswing.

He ran for a long time—it's hard to calculate time when your brain is fighting through flashing pain, but it was ten, fifteen minutes maybe. Then he stopped and dumped me on the ground.

I sprawled there, chest heaving, head throbbing with the blood rush from not hanging upside down anymore. A bright light raked across my blindfold, and I tucked into a ball. I didn't think I could stand on my own, let alone run—not until I'd recovered my breath. Where to run to? The blindfold was still secure, and my strapped hands were useless. I tried squinching my face to loosen the cloth.

The male voices were low—too low for me to understand, although I was pretty sure they weren't speaking English. Metallic clanks and then an engine roared to life, followed quickly by another in deafening tandem.

I was hoisted to standing and backed up and pushed onto a seat. A warm body crowded onto the seat with me, his arm tight around my waist. Then his muscles flinched, and we leaped forward.

ATVs, probably quads. They'd learned their lesson. I was pretty sure my captors were the finger-message people, just more of them and better equipped this time. And I'd made it easy for them.

But they'd taken only me. The boys were safe. Clarice. Walt. Sidonie, Hank and CeCe. Only me. It could have been so much worse.

I relaxed against the man's chest. If I'd known him in any other context, I would have thought his scent comforting—a mix of wood smoke, leather, motor oil, and cooked onions. It was like a record of what he'd been doing that day, before it came time to kidnap me.

I could try to throw myself off the ATV, but they'd probably stop, pick me up, and keep going. I needed all the wits and physical strength I could muster for what was coming next.

~oOo~

They stuffed me in a shallow place, small and hard, by the way their bumps and grunts echoed quickly. They removed the now soggy gob from my mouth and left me.

They didn't go far, though, because I could hear low voices and the occasional crackle of firewood sap igniting. I scooted in each direction until my shoulder bumped hard, cold wall on three sides, and a thick wood door on the fourth. I laid my cheek against the wall and felt the ridges of concrete block construction. Dampness seeped through the uneven floor.

They'd have never removed my gag if they thought my screaming would be a problem, which meant we were miles and miles from the nearest source of help. So I saved my breath and propped myself in a corner.

My mind was racing, but I wasn't coming to any conclusions. The cold got to me first—seeped into my aching muscles until time moved with agonizing slowness. Everything became stagnant—my heartbeat faded, the men's voices outside slurred, icy fingers crept over my limbs.

And I must have blacked out, or dozed, because slamming car doors jolted me to consciousness.

The door swung open, and someone pulled me to my feet. Pain prickles rampaged through my cramped legs as I staggered through the opening, the man prodding me in the back.

"Cut the ties," a surprisingly tenor voice said.

My arms were pulled down at an angle, and the bands popped off. I bit my tongue to keep from crying out as blood flooded into my hands. I flexed them carefully.

"I want to see her," said the same voice, and my blindfold was yanked off.

I squinted against the firelight, then slowly raised my eyes to the ring of faces of the men standing around the fire. No one I recognized. Dirt Bike Man was not part of the group, although most of the men could have been his siblings for similar appearance.

Except one. The shortest man separated himself from the group and strolled toward me. Light flickered off his rimless glasses. His hair was sandy brown and tightly curled close to his head. His eyes were lighter, hard to tell the color exactly in the dim, uneven firelight.

"So you're Nora Ingram," he said in the high-pitched voice that matched his stature.

"Nora Ingram-Sheldon," I corrected him.

He snickered, not a pleasant sound—nasal, almost wheezing. "I am Giuseppe Ricardo Solano."

"Numero Tres," I whispered.

He scowled. I think he would have preferred a higher rank. "I go by Joe."

He was dressed in an expensive pullover sweater—I guessed cashmere or very fine merino—and tailored slacks with wingtips. No wonder he'd had his henchmen do the dirty work of careening through the woods to abduct me. But he was broad-shouldered and thick through the torso with a crude toughness lurking below the designer clothes that was never developed in a boardroom. If he was scratched, he would bleed like a street hoodlum, his true colors.

"Since my men have been unable to locate your husband," Joe said, "I decided to pay you a visit."

"You *and* the FBI," I said, forcing bitterness into my voice. "Why does no one knock these days, or call first? Uncivilized." I glanced at the other four men who were clustered close to the fire but whom I suspected were also listening intently.

"What does the FBI know?" Joe's eyes narrowed behind his glasses.

"Less than they need to, more than they realize."

Joe barked an unamused laugh. "I might like you, Nora Ingram, which is a pity. Where's my money?"

"Are you a good Catholic?" I figured with a name like Giuseppe, his mother was, even if he wasn't.

Joe frowned slightly and rocked on his heels. "When it suits me."

"What's the going rate for a confession these days?"

"Ahh." A smug look crossed his face, and he cracked the knuckles of his left hand, flashing a glitzy pinkie ring in the process. "I thought you'd have something you wanted to tell me."

"You're the one who needs to confess. I've made the first payment on a get-out-of-purgatory layaway plan for you. Widows and orphans. Remember, Joe? I suspect you've made plenty of them when we're instructed, instead, to care for them." I stared at him.

"You'll get my money back." He made the statement flatly, as though the deed were already accomplished, and stepped closer.

I shook my head. "Too late. Your contribution is already well invested—on nutritious food for growing children and contractors for new dormitories and clean water wells and metal roofs and teachers and goats. Not the sort of currency you can recall."

Joe's fists balled at his sides and almost disappeared into the too-long, bunched-up sleeves of his sweater. His eyes glinted as he glared hard at me through his lowered pale lashes.

I arrowed my gaze straight back. No wavering—he must not see me flinch. He had to believe what I said was true—because it was true. I'd never be paying him back. He could kill me over the money if he wanted to, but that wouldn't make it reappear. But he might need to send a message to his associates in order to save face, just as he had with the fingerless subordinate. My heart was thumping so wildly, I was sure he could hear it.

He finally spoke through stiff lips, still frozen in his menacing stance. "You're more like your husband than I expected for being so recently married."

"What did he do for you, exactly?" I murmured.

"If you've been talking to the FBI, then you know," Joe snarled. "When I find him—and I will—I will kill him."

"Are you asking my permission?" I knew it was a smart aleck response and a huge risk, but I couldn't let him think I was beaten.

He whirled and smacked me across the cheek with the back of his fist. My neck snapped sideways and cracked, and I lost all feeling, all control. I fell flat, staring, my eyes dry. I couldn't even blink.

Feet walked past me, doors slammed, engines roared, and I was left in silence with the dying embers of the fire.

CHAPTER 23

Fog enveloped me like a down comforter, heavy, dense, and so thick I could barely see the junco hopping on the ground, scratching through pine needles to reach tasty morsels. His beady eye kept close watch on me, but I must not have stirred in long enough for him to feel safe.

He was joined by a mate, her head dusky charcoal in color. She reached my outspread fingers, pecked delicately around them, perched on my wrist for a fleeting second, then carried on with her foraging.

The thought that coyotes might be next prodded me into action. I pushed my torso up until I was sitting. Pine needles fell from where they'd been imprinted in my cheek. I was still in one piece, but I felt pulverized and jellied, with the screaming rush of a blinding migraine.

I doubled over, head between my knees, gulping huge breaths to hold back the nausea. The bird whistle Eli had given me swung forward on the leather thong around my neck, and I clutched it. My little bit of home. I was still alive.

I shouldn't be, but I was.

After a few experimental attempts, I balanced on my feet—hunched over with my hands propped on my knees, but progress at any rate. My body ached, dull and stiff.

I took a breather, and from that awkward position examined my surroundings, what wasn't masked by opaque fog. The cinder block hut that had been my prison stood like an outpost at the edge of a cultivated field that had not been tended recently. Bushy winter foliage mounded in overgrown, parallel rows. A dirt track ran by the hut's open door, with the ashy remnants of my captors' fire several yards away.

I went over last night's events in my mind, particularly our arrival—my stumbling, the direction I'd been shoved to get me in the hut—and decided we must have approached from the right.

I might as well be moving. I was cold to the core and starting to shiver. My fingers and toes were tingly lumps that I could barely wiggle.

I walked slowly, keeping to the road which had obviously been designed for tractor use only. Fog had frozen on the surface, dusting the dirt with a crunchy sugar coating like a fancy cupcake. The track took an abrupt turn at the corner of the field, and I stopped. I didn't remember any sharp turns on the ATV, but we'd probably been traveling cross-country.

I spun slowly, but the fog was a shifting white wall, making it impossible to get my bearings. Suddenly, the scent of toothpaste and cough drops filled the heavy air.

I glanced down—I'd stepped on a plant. I bent and crushed a leaf between my fingers and held them to my nose. The crop was peppermint.

The piercing freshness cleared my sinuses and maybe my brain, and I chuckled. Roads are built for a reason. I'd follow the road.

The only sound was my unsteady footsteps. I was grateful for the frozen ground—otherwise I'd have been slogging through mud. How long had I been gone? Clarice would have noticed when I didn't show up to help with the dishes. But then what?

I figured the best thing I could do was remember— remember everything possible about last night, about the men who'd taken me, about Numero Tres Joe and his operatives—what they'd looked like, what they'd said, why they'd spared me.

Why? I was still fuzzy about Joe's motives. Maybe he'd realized I was a dead end with regard to his money. Maybe he thought I was in contact with Skip and would pass along the threat against his life. Maybe he had to assess the situation for himself.

The news articles about him, while sketchy on specifics, had reported third-hand accounts of his tight-fisted management style, but had also said he tended to be reclusive, with hints of growing paranoia. Apparently the higher one rose in the cartel hierarchy, the greater the risk to one's life, from both outside and inside the organization.

Maybe Joe didn't think I'd survive in the wilderness by myself, that I was as good as dead anyway. Maybe he was right. My stomach rumbled, gnawing in on itself to remind me just how long it had been since my cozy family dinner.

I palmed Eli's gift and gave it a tentative puff. The same cheerful warble—and a comforting form of companionship.

The road didn't narrow but felt more closed in as it wound into increasingly dense trees that towered over me, their trunks puncturing and disappearing into the fog. The moisture in the air seemed to carry sounds—solitary chirps and scuttles as small animals went about their daily responsibilities.

If I could hear them, they could hear me. I could holler, but wasn't sure my voice would last long, or if anyone was looking for me. Or if they were looking for me, how would they find this patch of woods among the endless acres? I didn't even know if I was still in May County.

Or I could whistle. I might be mistaken for a bird, but I would be a very persistent and obnoxious bird.

~oOo~

Blowing on a whistle takes more tongue muscle—and saliva—than one would think. Hours later—two, three?—I was reduced to occasional squeaks, with long bouts of panting in between. It didn't help that the road was now a steep incline.

My flimsy efforts were becoming ridiculous. I flopped at the base of a tree and leaned against the trunk.

At least there was still a road. Miles and miles of road. Although at my pace I might have covered only a fraction of that distance. What distance? I had no idea.

I groaned and considered removing my boots to check on the blisters that were rising on my heels and left big toe. But the worry that I might not be able to get my boots back on kept me inert.

In ascending, I'd climbed into even thicker fog. I was tunneling through the middle of a cloud. I had no idea how many trees surrounded me now since I could see only the ones I could also touch.

Except for the road, I might have been walking in circles. There had been a few slight bends in the track, but I figured whoever put in the time and effort to build this road did so economically, diverting temporarily from the intended direction only for major obstacles that could not be removed.

For being visually impenetrable, the fog sure was fluid—swirling, pressing in on me, distorting even the shape of my own hands in my lap, confusing and lonely, the damp version of a mirage. And ruminating did no good for my situation.

I clawed my way up the tree until I was standing again and set out, one foot in front of the other.

Tweet.

Puff. Wheeze.

Chirp.

Pant.

The whistle and I developed an odd sort of syncopated cadence, but we carried on.

A branch crackled to my right, and I froze. Snap. Crunch.

Something was definitely walking toward me. It sounded big and heavy and clumsy. Not a cougar—didn't they have soft, padded feet? An elk? A bear? What other kinds of big, scary creatures roamed these hills? Sasquatch?

I peered into the fog, straining to see an antler rack or a bulky, mangy hide. If a wild animal and I bumped into each other and things got ugly, I knew who would win. But I couldn't take off running in the opposite direction because the road was my lifeline.

However, I could sound bigger and more intimidating than I was. I inhaled and gave a mighty blast on the whistle. It wasn't made to handle that much air all at once, and the resulting sound was a cross between a squealing pig and a sick chicken. Definitely scary. I blew again for good measure, expelling my entire lung capacity until the screech faded into a staccato gurgle.

A black form—no, two forms—two heads, four legs—came crashing through the brush and white vapor, assault rifles pointed at me.

I thrust my hands in the air and just about peed my pants.

"Nora Ingram?"

I emitted a tiny squeak that was supposed to be a yes.

"FBI. You alone?"

"Very," I whispered.

"You armed? They strap anything to you?"

I shook my head until my teeth rattled.

Another gigantic form came barreling out of the fog. I jumped out of the way, but not far enough as it squashed me in a suffocating hug.

"I knew it was you!"

His beard tickled my face, and I pushed back for speaking clearance. "Gus?" My voice wavered.

"I knew it was you." He beamed and gave me another squeeze that lifted me off the ground. "No real bird sounds like that. I knew it. Been trackin' you for a while, but these boys required some convincing to make their move. We couldn't tell if you were alone or on a forced march with the bad guys. Didn't want you gettin' hit in potential crossfire."

"You've been following me?" My mouth hung open. How could a three-hundred pound man stalk me through the woods without my hearing him?

"You wouldn't know it to look at me, but I was a Green Beret." Gus sighed and released me. "Back when I was a young buck."

"Thank you, thank you, thank you." I flung my arms around him this time. He chuckled and held me close. I buried my face in the bib of his overalls and sniffled against the denim.

Gus rubbed my back with his big, warm hands. "I knew somethin' was up when the feds came to town. Then yesterday's visitors just had drug cartel written all over them, and I started runnin' ideas together. Those bozos should know better than to drive a snazzy black Escalade in these parts. Stuck out like the thugs they are."

"You need medical attention?" one of the FBI men asked.

I tried to smile through my tears. "I'll soak my feet when I get home."

"Your face doesn't look too good." He gently placed a thumb on the edge of my jaw and turned my head to the side. "Who hit you?"

"Giuseppe Ricardo Solano."

The FBI agent's brows arched, and he slid my sleeves up a few inches, exposing the raw gouges in my wrists from the straps. His serious brown eyes returned to meet mine. "You're lucky."

"I know," I whispered.

"She's also shakin' like a leaf," Gus said. "Let's get her warm."

CHAPTER 24

They radioed ahead and hiked me a short distance, where we were met by a windowless cargo van and driver. At the command post, they wrapped me in blankets and poured coffee from a thermos into a foam cup for me. I took a sip and scalded the roof of my mouth. I made a little nest with the edge of a blanket so I could hold the cup without exposing my fingers to the chilly air.

More members of the extraction team materialized. They all looked the same—dark clothes from head to foot, helmets, assault rifles, radios. And they'd been looking for me. I suddenly felt very small.

I gathered from their banter as they stashed their gear that Gus had suspected where I was being held because he'd seen taillights on the track to the mint field and knew the farmer had no reason to be checking on his dormant crop at dusk in the middle of winter.

And Gus had seen the taillights only because he'd been at one of his favorite viewpoints all afternoon, before the fog rolled in. He'd been scanning the skies for a peregrine falcon he was worried about since he hadn't seen her overhead for a few days. Gus was getting ribbed by the men in black for his hobby, and he quietly shuffled out of the group.

He sidled up to the van's open side door where I was huddled in a passenger captain's chair. "Her name's Mattie. Short for Matilda. She probably wouldn't like that name, but it was the best I could come up with. As close as I can tell, she's eleven or twelve years old, has raised fledglings on a cliff face a few miles north of town the past several years."

"Just Mattie, or do you keep tabs on other birds too?" I asked.

"376," Gus said proudly. "That's my life list count so far. Not many, but I figure I have a few more years to add to the total."

"That's crazy."

Gus sighed. "Some people collect postage stamps, but that was too easy, considerin' what I do for a livin'. So I decided to collect bird sightings. I suppose it is crazy, but the hunt has its talons in me now." He shrugged.

"I meant crazy good. That's amazing." I wriggled an arm free from the blankets and squeezed his shoulder. "Thanks for your vigilance and keeping tabs on me too."

"What are neighbors for, 'cept to be nosy?" Gus winked at me.

Matt joined our tête-à-tête, his hands stuffed deep in the pockets of his overcoat.

"I didn't know you were here," I said.

"I found someone else to babysit the lab work. Unfortunately, you're my responsibility, and I hate it when my charges get kidnapped."

"Happen often?"

"Nope. You ready to go?"

"Can I keep the blankets?"

Matt's grim look lightened a little. "Sure." He ushered me into the backseat of a nearby sedan.

Violet joined Matt in the front, and he eased the big car onto the paved road. The backseat was broad and cushy and I was incredibly tempted to tip over and doze, but I wanted to see where I was. Every once in a while, I felt Matt's eyes on me in the rearview mirror.

While none of us spoke, icy resentment rolled off Violet in waves, as though my involuntary escapade had inconvenienced her at a most inopportune time. Matt relaxed in the driver's seat, his knees almost touching the steering wheel, and he corrected the car with minor touches of his thumbs and forefingers.

After half an hour of curvy country roads, the area started looking familiar. Then we rolled through the intersection between the store and post office, the hum of the sedan's tires on the pavement providing lulling background noise.

Matt zipped past the secret gate to Mayfield. I leaned forward, my hand on the back of his seat, my mouth open to point out his error.

"We're going to the Gonzales's place," he said with a quick glance in the mirror.

"Is something wrong?"

He shook his head. "Clarice insisted. Said it'd be easiest to keep an eye on you there, since she's also watching after the little girl."

"What about Sidonie?" I blurted. "That means—"

"Mrs. Gonzales went into labor shortly after everyone realized you were missing," Matt said matter-of-factly.

I groaned and slumped back against the seat.

Violet shifted and spoke for the first time. "She was due any second as it was. She'll be fine. She strikes me as the sturdy sort."

I glared at the back of Violet's head.

Clarice greeted us in front of a clapboard-sided, boxy ranch house with peeling gray paint. She had the tiny hand of a tutu-clad CeCe clasped tightly in her own. She pulled me in for a long hug with her free arm.

"I'm saving the lecture for later," Clarice said.

"Thanks." I chucked CeCe under the chin, and the little girl beamed at me. "Any word?"

"Hank promised to call once the ordeal's over." Clarice's hints at subtlety are hardly that.

"It's probably a good thing you skipped over motherhood and went straight to grandmotherhood," I said, smiling into Clarice's eyes.

She chuckled and pirouetted a delighted CeCe. "No doubt."

"Shall we?" Violet lugged a briefcase out of the car and strode toward the house with it banging against the side of her thigh.

Clarice sneered and rolled her eyes, but turned and followed Violet with CeCe tippy-toeing in her wake.

We entered the kitchen, passed a table littered with sheets of paper covered with tic-tac-toe grids and homemade dot-to-dot drawings and the leftovers of an egg salad sandwich, carrot stick, and peanut butter cookie lunch, and settled in a cozy living room with antimacassars draped over the backs and arms of every overstuffed piece of furniture.

Clarice announced her intention to read stories, and CeCe happily shadowed her down a narrow hallway, leaving me with the two FBI agents.

Violet set a recorder on the coffee table, clicked it on, and propped an open notebook on the arm of her chair. I tucked my legs under me on the sofa and folded my hands in my lap.

Matt's serious look was back. "Let's go through your past twenty-four hours."

So that's what we did—forward, backward, chronologically, random impressions, descriptions of every man in the party, descriptions of vehicles and ATVs, the cinder block hut, word-for-word repetitions of what each person said, my decision to start walking instead of waiting to be found.

I riled at his insinuation that I had hindered the rescue by leaving the scene. "How was I to know you were coming? I considered it very likely I would freeze out there, and I had a road to follow."

"How could you think we wouldn't come?" Matt's jaw clenched.

"Remember when I asked for protection?"

His eyes narrowed. "The situation's changed."

"I'd like to know why I was let off easy."

"Easy?" Matt's brows shot up. "Forcible abduction is not an outcome we were hoping for." He exhaled and ran a hand through the short hair on the back of his head. "Solano—Joe, as you call him—is under pressure from his bosses. They do that—put the screws on subordinates, all the way down the line. Reports are they're not thrilled about how much money he lost by trusting Skip, nor are they pleased with how he handled the hit on Rojas. It appears that his judgment in general has been called into question by his superiors, which does not bode well for his longevity, either professional or personal. He might have thought your dead body would be one too many on his résumé just now."

"But he could have killed me and left me." I leaned forward, elbows on knees. "Who knows how long it would have been until someone found me."

Matt blew out an exasperated sigh. "Are you going to argue about this?"

I smiled ruefully and shook my head. "Why did the agent who found me ask if they'd strapped anything to me?"

Matt slumped in his chair, his head tilted against the padded back, his eyes directed toward the ceiling.

Violet glanced at him and frowned. "Because they've been known to booby-trap their victims with suicide vests. That way, they take out their target and maybe a few law enforcement personnel at the same time."

I bit my lip. It was a good thing I hadn't known that earlier. "Do you know where Joe is now?"

"We have all his known haunts under surveillance." Violet retrieved the recorder and packed her things in the briefcase.

In other words, no, they didn't know where Joe was. On the other hand, I doubted he'd return any time soon. The more pressure he faced in his own business, the less I expected he'd interfere with mine. Maybe I could help keep it that way.

"I'll be careful," I said.

"You ever hear of D.B. Cooper?" Matt asked in a lazy voice from his still reclined position.

"No." I frowned.

"You'd have been too young to remember. Hijacker who jumped out of a Northwest Airlines plane in 1971 with $200,000 in ransom money. He was supposed to have landed around here." He stood and buttoned his coat. "I'm just saying you never know what you might encounter in these woods. You need to be more than careful, Nora. We'll work out a security detail for you."

At least he hadn't suggested I return to the city. I preferred my guardian angels in the form of Etherea and Gus.

I showed Matt and Violet to the door then crept softly down the hall. I found Clarice sitting cross-legged on the floor beside a pint-sized bed, leafing through an Olivia the Pig book. CeCe was out cold, resting on her side with her arm under her head, snoring softly as though just minutes ago she'd been peering over Clarice's shoulder at the pictures.

"Learning anything?" I whispered.

Clarice shot me a glare, closed the book, and slowly pushed to standing, her knees cracking so loudly I checked CeCe for eyelash flutters. But the little girl slept on. Clarice covered CeCe with a Winnie the Pooh fleece blanket and flapped her hand to urge me away from the doorway.

After she clicked the bedroom door closed, she muttered, "Why didn't they have books like that when I was a kid? I would have read more."

I kept Clarice company while she punched down the rising pizza dough for dinner.

"Don't you want to sleep?" she asked.

I shrugged. "I can do that later. Tell me about everyone."

"We all went sort of panicky once we figured out you were gone, and the FBI wouldn't let us help, just kept asking us a bunch of dumb questions we didn't know the answers to. Then that fellow, Gus, called and asked after you. When he heard you were missing, he barged in and took over. Never seen such a flurry." Clarice set her hands on her hips and scowled in admiration.

"Walt and the boys?" I asked.

"Sick with worry. Last I saw, Walt and a few of the older boys were on the roof, cleaning our chimneys."

I groaned.

"Seems that man takes his emotions out in his work. Also seems he thinks we're going to be burning a truckload of wood pellets this winter."

"I suppose we could, to keep up appearances. We'd have to find another place to stash the cash." I frowned.

"Maybe you should tell him the truth." Clarice squinted at me from behind her cat's-eye glasses.

"At what cost?" I whispered.

"He's a grown man. Try trusting him."

The phone hanging on the wall rang, loud and shrill. Clarice and I both jumped and stared at it. Then we lunged for it at the same time. Clarice beat me to it.

"Uh-huh. Just fine, yes. Right. Yes." She was nodding vigorously.

I poked her arm. "What?"

She waved me off. "Uh-huh. Got that. You rest now. Hug Sidonie for us. Yes, both of us. Nora's here. We're all fine. Uh-huh. Bye-bye."

"What?" I hollered.

"Shhhh," Clarice hissed, pointing in the direction of CeCe's back bedroom, but she was beaming. "Adam and Aron. Over seven pounds each. Healthy and hungry. Sidonie's elated."

"More boys," I murmured.

"Just what we need." Clarice returned to the stove and the simmering tomato sauce.

~oOo~

CeCe and I gobbled down pizza slices—sausage and olive for me, Hawaiian for her—in feminine solidarity. Given the fact that two more boys had just entered the world, and this household, we girls were going to have to stick together.

CeCe conscripted me into a game of Chutes and Ladders while Clarice cleaned up the dishes. I had just been dumped back to the bottom of the board by a nasty spin on the dial when a knock sounded.

Clarice wiped her hands on her apron and cracked open the kitchen door. "Didn't fall off, then?" she grunted.

"What? Oh. No, we're fine." Walt craned his head through the opening and grinned at me. "Nora. It's good to see you."

I grinned back. "I like your haircut."

He ran a hand over his bristly top thatch self-consciously. "It's growing on me." Then he cast a quick glance at Clarice's backside. She was leaning over the sink again, elbow-deep in sudsy water. "Um, can I talk to you for a few minutes?"

I grabbed a towel and handed it to CeCe. "Help Clarice?" I asked with a wink.

CeCe scooted off her chair with a broad smile.

Outside, Walt said, "I'm really glad to see you. I wasn't sure—we didn't know—I wish I could have prevented—"

"Shhh." I turned to him. "No regrets, no what-ifs. It's over, and I was spared." I shook my head. "I don't know why, but I was."

"I know why." Walt tipped up my chin so he was looking straight into my eyes. "You have too many people to take care of. Eli said so, and you know he's never wrong."

His cheeks were chapped and flushed, probably from being on the mansion roof in this cold weather, but his eyes were happy, even sparkly in the light cast from the kitchen window.

"So I can stay at Mayfield?" I asked.

"Where else would you flee, but to our old bastion of refuge? I'm afraid you're stuck with us."

But I didn't feel stuck. I felt at home—right here among friends—with Walt the practical poet standing so close I could feel the warmth radiating off him.

Walt's tone changed. "We have a little problem."

"What?"

"Come see." He slipped his hand over mine and led me to Bertha.

Three boys—Thomas, Dill, and Eli—were crowded in the cab with a limp but lumpy black plastic garbage bag spread across their laps.

"We found it—"

"No, I found it—"

"Maybe because we haven't taken the garbage to the dump in a while."

"But how did it get out to the Terminator?"

"I think Orville did it—"

"Or Wilbur. You know he roots through the trash when he can."

"Maybe he snuck into the mansion again."

I held up a hand. "What's in the bag?"

Dill cautiously peeled back the opening to reveal, in the dim overhead light of the cab, a hideous, hairy pelt of familiar mushroom color.

The Margaret Thatcher lookalike headpiece. I gasped.

"Is she gonna be mad?" Eli whispered. "Because the Terminator was chewing on it, and it's kind of messed up."

Kind of was an understatement. I lifted the snarled, saliva-ed hairball with just my fingertips.

And then I was giggling uncontrollably. "No," I said, "Clarice is not going to mind. But I think it'd be better if we didn't tell her." I made eye contact with each solemn boy, then winked. "Let's just pretend this never happened."

WHAT'S NEXT

GRAB & GO
Mayfield Mystery #2

When Nora Ingram-Sheldon learns her fugitive criminal husband had (has?) his crooked fingers in even more May County, Washington businesses, and that his involvement puts her new friends and neighbors at risk, what can she do but go on the hunt—for answers, for culprits, and for cracks she can widen in his many-tentacled money laundering enterprise?

But an omnipresent FBI security detail puts a damper on her movements, plus she's supposed to be a good example for the band of misfit boys in foster care at Mayfield's poor farm.

Maybe undercover is the way to go. Can she sneak away from her faithful executive assistant, Clarice, and Walt Neftali, the boys' guardian?

The tricky part is finding and putting her husband's gangster clients out of commission before they do the same to her.

NOTES & ACKNOWLEDGMENTS

Woodland and Longview are both real cities along the I-5 corridor in southwest Washington State. However, I have taken tremendous liberties with spacing and locations, and all the retail establishments and institutions, including county government, described in the Mayfield series are entirely fictional and placed for the convenience of storytelling. If you decide to visit the area, though, I can promise you will find just as many trees, mountains, backroads, and neighborly folks—and as much rain—as described.

Profound thanks to the following people who gave their time and expertise to assist in the writing of this series:

Debra Biaggi and BJ Thompson, beta readers extraordinaire.

Sergeant Fred Neiman, Sr. and all the instructors of the Clark County Sheriff's Citizens' Academy. The highlights had to be firing the Thompson submachine gun and stepping into the medical examiner's walk-in cooler. Oh, and the K-9 demonstration and the officer survival/lethal force decision making test. And the drug task force presentation with identification color spectrum pictures and the—you get the idea.

I claim all errors, whether accidental or intentional, solely as my own.

Deepest gratitude to *everyone* who reads my books—but most especially to those readers who take the time to post reviews online. Your comments continue to make a world of difference, not just for me as an author, but also for all the other readers out there who are considering what new mystery series to dive into.

I also have a monthly newsletter in which I share about writing progress, ask for reader input, run the occasional contest or giveaway, and just generally enthuse about books. If that sounds like your cup of tea, you can sign up at my website: jerushajones.com

ABOUT THE AUTHOR

Jerusha writes cozy mystery series which are set along the rivers and amid the forests of her beloved Pacific Northwest. She spends most of her time seated in front of her attic window, engaged in daydreaming with intermittent typing or pinning Post-It notes to corkboards (better safe than sorry!). She also considers maple-frosted, cream-filled doughnuts an essential component of her writer's toolkit.

She posts updates on her website: jerushajones.com

If you'd like to be notified about new book releases, please sign up for her email newsletter on her website. Your email address will never be shared, swapped, or sold and you can unsubscribe at any time.

She loves hearing from readers via email at jerusha@jerushajones.com

ALSO BY JERUSHA JONES

Imogene Museum Mystery Series
Rock Bottom
Doubled Up
Sight Shot
Tin Foil
Faux Reel
Shift Burn
Stray Narrow

Sockeye County Mystery Series
Sockeye County Shorts
Sockeye County Briefs
Sockeye County Au Naturel
Sockeye County Skinny

Jericho McElroy Mystery Series
The Double-Barreled Glitch

Tin Can Mystery Series
Mercury Rising
Silicon Waning
Carbon Dating
Silver Lining
Lead Flying
Oxygen Burning
Iron Sinking
Neon Warning

Mayfield Mystery Series
Bait & Switch
Grab & Go
Hide & Find
Cash & Carry
Tried & True

Made in the USA
Columbia, SC
26 September 2020